Also by Jamie Sumner

Roll with It
Tune It Out

ONE KID'S TRASH

JAMIE SUMNER

 ATHENEUM BOOKS FOR YOUNG READERS
New York   London   Toronto   Sydney   New Delhi

𝒜
atheneum

ATHENEUM BOOKS FOR YOUNG READERS

An imprint of Simon & Schuster Children's Publishing Division

1230 Avenue of the Americas, New York, New York 10020

For information about special discounts for bulk purchases, please contact Simon & Schuster Special Sales at 1-866-506-1949 or business@simonandschuster.com.

The Simon & Schuster Speakers Bureau can bring authors to your live event. For more information or to book an event, contact the Simon & Schuster Speakers Bureau at 1-866-248-3049 or visit our website at www.simonspeakers.com.

Interior design by Karyn Lee

The text for this book was set in Amasis MT.

Manufactured in the United States of America

0721 FFG

First Edition

10 9 8 7 6 5 4 3 2 1

Library of Congress Cataloging-in-Publication Data

Names: Sumner, Jamie, author.

Title: One kid's trash / Jamie Sumner.

Description: First edition. | New York : Atheneum Books for Young Readers, [2021] | Audience: Ages 10 and Up. | Summary: When his father moves them halfway across Colorado, eleven-year-old Hugo "Shorts" O'Donnell is surprised that his remarkable talent for garbology makes him popular for the first time in his life.

Identifiers: LCCN 2020046451 | ISBN 9781534457034 (hardcover) | ISBN 9781534457058 (ebook)

Subjects: CYAC: Bullying—Fiction. | Popularity—Fiction. | Middle schools—Fiction. | Schools—Fiction. | Moving, Household—Fiction.

Classification: LCC PZ7.1.S8545 One 2021 | DDC [Fic]—dc23

LC record available at https://lccn.loc.gov/2020046451

To Dad—
Love you. Race you to the bottom.

And for the kids who've ever been bullied—
I feel you. Be brave. Be better than them.

Chapter One

....

The Coefficient of Hugo

The beautiful and terrible thing about having your bedroom in the basement is that you never know what time it is. So when Mom yells down the stairs, "Hugo, if you don't get up this minute, you will miss the bus!" I assume that I am already late. And if I miss the bus, there is only one other option: Mom drives me. Which isn't really an option at all. I am not having my mother drive me to the first day of middle school. That's social suicide. A guy like me can't afford to take chances.

I sprint to the bathroom and take the fastest shower in the history of showers. And then I run up the stairs with socks in my mouth and my arms full of jacket, shoes, and backpack. Mom takes one look at me in the hallway and says, "You can't go out with your hair wet."

I spit the socks onto the floor.

"Either I catch the bus, or I dry my hair. You can't have it both ways, Mom."

I start yanking on a sock, slightly damp from my mouth. Mom watches in her pink fuzzy bathrobe. Back home she was the first one up and dressed and out the door. She had her own private therapy practice in an office building downtown. Client appointments started at eight a.m., which I never understood. If I could set my own schedule, nothing would begin before eleven.

She crouches down and hands me my other sock. Then she reaches out like she's going to fix my hair. It's shooting in a million different directions. I bob and weave like a boxer.

"Mom. No."

"Okay, I just— Do you have your phone?"

The phone is new. They said I couldn't have one until I turned twelve, which isn't until April, but I guess with the move they thought I'd need it sooner. So uprooting my entire life came with *one* bonus.

"Yeah, I got it." I stand and grab my bag.

"Here, take this." She tosses me a chocolate PediaSure.

"No. Uh-uh." I throw it back to her like a hot potato. "I'm too old for this."

"You're only too old when Dr. Ross says you're too old." She stuffs the bottle in my bag.

Dr. Ross is my pediatrician. She's had me on a weight-gain plan since, well, when I came out of the womb two months too soon. I bet I've drunk approximately four thousand shakes. "Creamy" chocolate, "French" vanilla, "very berry" strawberry—they all taste like chalk. And they don't work . . . obviously. I'm the dot on the growth chart that can't reach a line. I'm Ant-Man if he couldn't unshrink himself. My aunt once bought me age-appropriate athletic shorts for my birthday. They came to my shins. Adam, the meanest kid in second grade, took one look at me and said, "Nice pants, Shorts." That was my name for the next two years. *Please, please, please,* I say to the universe as I head out the door, *don't let me be Shorts again.* The universe probably isn't listening. I bet it doesn't take client calls until eleven.

"Text if you need *anything*, okay?" Mom says. I sigh but give her a side hug as Dad comes skidding down the hall at a run.

He's in jeans and he's fighting the zipper on his Patagonia jacket. The zipper seems to be winning. It's weird to see him without a tie. "Come on, I'll walk you to—" He checks his watch. "Er, we'll jog to the bus stop." That's the other new thing. We sold Mom's Tahoe to help save money while she builds up her practice again and Dad does . . . whatever Dad plans to do. Now he has to catch the bus, just like me. Except his bus carries him to his new job in Creekside, the resort town at the top of the mountain, and mine takes me to purgatory—I mean, middle school.

I follow him out the door. His hair may be a totally different color, carroty red compared to my dark brown, but it looks just as bad as mine—permanent bedhead. Outside, the wind is fierce and yellow birch leaves dart through the air like angry hummingbirds. It's only the beginning of September, but you can smell the cold coming.

We jog toward the end of the block and then break into a sprint when the bus passes us on its way to the corner. It screeches to a halt in a cloud of exhaust—the little engine that couldn't—and I barely make it before it chugs off again. This is good. I'm so late I don't have time to be nervous. I hurl myself into the heat of the bus before the doors whoosh closed behind me. I dart up the steps as fast as I can, praying for invisibility. But when I turn down the aisle, the bus driver says, "Hey, little fella, there's plenty of room up front." She points to the empty seat right behind her. *Little fella.* Two girls across the aisle giggle. I don't even dare to look at anybody else. I walk all the way to an unoccupied row near the back. Outside on the sidewalk, Dad waves and waves and waves. I ignore him and blink back the tears that could only make this situation worse.

And so it begins.

Beech Creek Middle School looks a lot like every other public school in the universe. When we pull into the circle,

I take my time filing out and give the place a nervous once-over. It's a brick, one-story building, one long Lego, except it has stone columns in front of the main entrance—an attempt to be as classy as the resort up the hill. But it's just a game of dress-up. If you live down here, you're not a part of that world. Anybody rich enough to actually *live* in a lodge/chalet/palace up on high goes to the private school outside Vail.

How do I know this, as the new kid? My cousin Vijay, Vij, also lives here and goes to Beech Creek. He gave me the lowdown on the who, what, when, and where of the place. He was trying to help, but every conversation ended with me hanging up the phone and gently banging my head against the window of the bedroom in Denver that I did not want to leave. Trying to fit into a new school is like studying for a test for a class you've never taken.

It took me until fourth grade to make any friends worth keeping—Jason and Marquis and Cole, who are probably already searching for my FIFA replacement. Marquis was the first one to show me how to double tap the shoot button at the right time. I scored some sublime goals because of him. He's also the first one who invited me over for game night and introduced me to Jason and Cole and their intense love for spray cheese. I will not miss the cheese, but I will miss them.

I hitch my backpack up on my shoulders. Vij waits for me by the main entrance. He's wearing sunglasses even though the sky is one long blanket of cloud, and he's throwing a bouncy ball over and over against one of the stone columns. He looks like he's been here his whole life. I wish I had that level of confidence about *anything*.

"Hey," I say, and duck as the bouncy ball goes careening off the stone, over my head, and into the street.

Vij lets it go.

"Hey, dude. You ready?" He lifts his glasses and his eyebrows at the same time. I'm not ready. Of course I'm not, but what am I going to do, hide under the cars with the bouncy ball? I take a deep breath and let him lead me inside.

I do not make eye contact with a single person. My stomach sloshes with Cinnamon Toast Crunch and nerves. Vij high-fives everyone, including the secretary, who hands me my schedule and *ruffles my hair* on my way to first period. I blush and keep my eyes trained on the ground. Females find my smallness irresistible, but in the worst way possible. I am a potential pet.

I have English first with Vij, who directs us both to the back corner near the window. Because this is the first day of middle school for the entire sixth grade, I assumed everyone else would be stunned into submission, like me, by the boatload of newness. But they all already know one another because they went to elementary school together. It's like trying to join a team when the positions are already filled. I wait, slightly behind Vij, while he does the whole "hey, this is my cuz, be nice to him" thing. I love my cousin. But I wish I didn't need a tour guide for my own life. I smile shyly at the floor and ignore the girls who whisper "isn't he cute" because I know they don't mean "cool." They mean "adorable," like a puppy they want to carry around. No guy wants to be adorable. Ever.

Vij takes the last seat in the row, leaving the one right in front of him open for me. I sit and do what I've been doing since first grade: slouch down in my seat so you can't tell exactly how short I really am. I wouldn't have been the king of the school by a long shot, but at least if I'd stayed in Denver I would have still had my friends, the ones who let me have the lowest swing on the playground without making a big deal about it and came over to play Xbox all summer and basically forgot I was *little* Hugo and just thought of me as Hugo. I watch everyone else out of the corner of my eye. They already know who to sit with and what color one another's walls are at home and what movies they saw this summer. Like the new Marvel movie me and Jason and Marquis and Cole saw in the dine-in theater before I left. We ate nachos and drank slushies and laughed at all the bad superhero lines.

During roll call, I nudge Vij when they call his name, because he's already not listening. He stares out the window, totally engrossed in the plight of a Doritos bag blowing across the parking lot. Our English teacher, Mrs. Jacobsen, says his name sharply, like fingers snapping, over and over until he mumbles "here." She wears square red glasses that she pushes up on her head and then can't find when they get lost in her curly hair during her PowerPoint. She seems all right, but kind of scary in that "I can do the crossword puzzle in eight seconds" way. Her syllabus is twelve pages long, front *and* back. I didn't even know what a syllabus was until today. Lucky for me, she included the definition on page one.

Vij and I split up for second period. I talk to no one, look at no one, and say exactly two words: "yes, ma'am" when my Spanish teacher, Señora Molitoris, asks me if I'm settling in okay. I'm so relieved to see Vij when we meet again for third period that I have to stop myself from hugging him. Then the bell rings and Mr. Wahl, our algebra teacher, slams the door like he's locking in the prisoners. A gloom settles over the room that has nothing to do with the clouds outside. I shiver.

There's always *one* class where the goal is simply to survive. You're not aiming for As or Bs or to make a new best friend. You just want to get through. As the seconds tick by and Mr. Wahl stares at the class, saying nothing, not even *blinking*, I realize this is my survival class. My throat fills with cotton. I couldn't swallow even if I wanted to, which I don't, because I am already terrified of drawing his laser eyes toward me.

The first, and nicest thing, I can say about Mr. Wahl is that at least he's color coordinated. Which is to say, he wears entirely one hue: tan. Tan shirt tucked into tan pants that are just short enough to reveal tan socks. His hair is the same washed-out brown as his shoes. The only spark of color on him is a green notepad sticking out of his shirt pocket. It is a packet of detention slips.

He doesn't call roll. Instead, he passes a sheet of paper down the aisle, and we're supposed to check ourselves off a list. I'm pretty sure he isn't planning on talking at all, or you know, trying to match actual faces with names. Vij, who is sitting behind me again, decides this is excellent.

"Man, you think he even counts heads?" he whispers. "I could put a mop in this seat, and he wouldn't notice." He looks out the window again. I follow his gaze. He's staring at the road that leads up the mountain. It's lined with flags of all the countries of the world. It's Creekside's royal welcome to ski country.

"Uh-uh. No way." I shake my head.

"What?" he says in the voice he uses when his mom asks if he's the reason his little sister is crying.

"There's not even snow yet, Vijay. We can't skip school to go skiing. Our parents will murder us and then host a double funeral-slash-family reunion."

"We're not skipping school, man. I swear." He scowls at me like I'm the buzzkill of the century. "And don't call me 'Vijay.' You sound like my mother."

"You. Back right." Mr. Wahl's voice lashes out from the front of the room like a whip. "What's your name?"

"O'Connell, sir," Vij says, the "sir" sounding more like a curse.

"And you." He points at me. "Name."

"O'Connell."

He walks halfway up our aisle. Behind all that tan, he's younger than he looks. I shrink down farther in my seat.

"Is this a joke?"

"No, sir," I say now, because Vij is ignoring us both and studying his hands like they hold the mystery of the universe. "We're cousins."

Mr. Wahl looks back and forth between us. I can see him comparing Vij's brown skin and my pasty white face and weighing the odds. Then he shakes his head and stalks back to the front of the room.

"Mr. Vijay O'Connell, what's the coefficient of $10x - 8$?"

"The ten," Vij says without looking up. He's pulled out a Sharpie and is tracing the lines on his palm like a spiderweb. Mr. Wahl blinks. Because Vij never acts like he cares about school, nobody expects him to know anything. But he's supersmart and he doesn't even have to try. Same with making friends. He's always been able to just *do* things. It's never bothered me before. In fact, I was proud of him. But it's different hearing about it on Christmas vacations and summer visits over a campfire. Up close and personal, it's . . . annoying. Now that we're in the same school and wading in the same small pond of people, I kind of wish Vij were a slightly smaller, slightly dumber version of himself. Then I feel bad for thinking that because he's using all his social superpowers to smooth the way for me. I should be totally grateful to have him here. As Mom loves to say when I refuse to brush my hair, *you only get one chance to make a first impression*, and Vij is the best chance I've got to get it right.

In the cafeteria, I clutch my sack lunch and follow him past the guys in athletic wear—the snowboard, basketball, track crowd, which I assumed (and dreaded) were Vij's people. Instead, we walk to a table near the windows with just four people. There is not a single Smith or Under Armour logo in sight. Vij points at two guys, both with white-blond hair and freckles, so identical that they have to be twins, and says, "Jackson, Grayson, meet my cousin, Hugo."

"Jack," Jackson says.

"Gray," Grayson says.

I wave. I will never be able to tell them apart.

The kid at my elbow chirps, "I'm Micah!" He has brown

hair and glasses with an actual strap across the back. He blinks at me with eyes magnified to unnatural proportions. I recognize him from algebra class. I'm ashamed to admit I singled him out immediately as a potential weaker link than me. While I am shorter than almost any eleven-year-old on the planet, there's something about Micah that just *feels* small.

"Do you want my milk? The lunch lady gave me two!" he asks, each sentence ending higher than it started.

I smile and shake my head. "No, thanks." I would bet a thousand bucks he still sleeps in matching pajamas and uses a light-up toothbrush to tell him how long before he can spit. But at least he doesn't make me nervous. In fact, this is the first time today that my heart has decided to beat at a normal pace. I might even be able to eat my lunch.

I sneak a look at the end of the table to the girl who has not lifted her head—the only one I haven't met.

Vij sits down opposite the twins and pulls me down with him. "That," he says, "is Em."

"Emilia," she corrects him while typing on her phone at approximately 1,783 words per minute.

"So you're the new kid from Denver," Jack says. Or Gray.

I nod and unwrap my peanut butter and banana sandwich only to discover that my mom has cut it in the shape of a heart. I tear it to pieces as fast as I can, but not before Vij sees.

"Shut up," I say before he can laugh.

He unsnaps the lid on his own lunch with a flourish. Micah leans over me to see. It's orange and looks like cat vomit. I make a grab for it.

"Get your hands off."

"Is that your mom's curry?" I ask.

Aunt Soniah makes the best curry on the planet. This is a fact. She should get a medal for it. Maybe she has. I wouldn't be surprised. It is creamy and gingery and just the right amount of spicy I have dreams about this curry.

While we all watch, Vij unbends the metal spoon attached to the lid like a pocketknife and takes a huge bite. This is what makes Vij impressive. Most kids would be embarrassed to have a lunch that smelled of anything other than pizza or Doritos. But Vij doesn't care. Careless. Carefree. Envy knits a stitch in my side.

I stare down at my lunch like it's toilet paper I trailed in on my shoes—a heart torn to pieces and a note from Mom that says "Good luck on your first day! Remember, deep breaths!" It's humiliating. What sixth grader still gets notes in his lunch? I should throw it away, but I stuff it in my pocket instead. I like knowing it's there. You would have to make me eat a hundred heart-shaped sandwiches before I'd admit it, though.

Micah shoves his lunch tray under my nose. "You can have some of my spaghetti. I have breadsticks!"

After I politely decline, Vij waves his hand over the table like the host on *Jeopardy!* and says, "This, my cuz, is the newspaper staff." He shoots a finger at me. "You, too, could be a part of the dream team."

"The, uh, what?"

"Did no one tell you?" Vij pretends to be shocked. "*News flash*: This crew is going to be responsible for the very first newspaper in Beech Creek history."

Micah gnaws on a breadstick. The twins trade chips. Emilia types. This has to be Vij's mom's idea. She's always penciling in extracurriculars for his future resume. It's not easy having two older sisters in Ivy League schools and a younger one who reads the dictionary for fun. An afternoon at Vij's house makes me glad I'm an only child.

Vij bumps my shoulder with his. "You ready to make history, man?"

"Ummm." It's not like I had dreams of being cool. Mom always talks about the importance of setting "attainable goals." Coolness is *not* an attainable goal for me. And I've come to terms with it. But this is the *opposite* of that. Joining the newspaper staff would be like pinning a bullseye on my back and then passing out flyers advertising free target practice. Suddenly, I am much less comfortable at this table.

"Here it is!" Emilia yells, holding up her phone and rescuing me from Vij's stare. I could hug her, except she looks like the kind that can and will throw a punch.

"Let me see," Jack or Gray says.

Emilia passes over her phone. The twins say "uhhh?" together at the exact same time. "Give it, Jack," Vij says, and takes it from the twin with the scar over his eyebrow. I make a mental note.

"Ummm, no offense, Em, but what am I looking at here?" he asks.

Emilia comes around the table to stand behind us.

"That's a picture of the parking lot!" she informs us.

"Well, yes. And?" Emilia grabs the phone from him and swipes left, hard.

"*And* . . . this is the same red Volvo in the handicapped spot without proper licensure," she adds, holding it up an inch from his face.

She watches us and waits. For what, I have no idea. When we just sit there, she yanks her ponytail tighter and sighs like my mom.

"That's *illegal*," she explains.

I know it's a huge mistake before it happens, but everyone knows you can't stop an eye roll midroll. When she catches me, her glare could melt bones.

"What a lovely addition to our table," she quips. "Thanks a lot, Vij."

So, if we're rating things on a first-day scale, similar to the pain scale at the doctor's office, one being "I am now king of the school" and ten being "I have to change my name and relocate ASAP," English and Spanish were solid fours—not terrible, mostly tolerable. Algebra is teetering on a seven with the specter of Mr. Wahl looming for the next nine months. Lunch would have been a three (I ate with other humans who did not try to see if I fit in the trash can), except for the newspaper invite, which will get me thrown in a trash can, so I'm sitting at a solid seven. Emilia would probably say eleven.

But none of that matters, because I am about to enter the most painful part of all: physical education. Gym is the foundation on which the house of bullying was built. *Hey kid, you're about eye-level with everyone else's elbow, right? Let's shoot some hoops. Your legs are half the size of everyone else's? Go line up. It's relay races. Tug-of-war? We'll put you in the middle where you can dangle like dead weight. Not even enough dead weight to count.*

The locker room reeks of sweat and farts and floor varnish. I find my name along the row. Vij's locker is on the other side of the room, so I'm standing by myself, trying to shove my sweatshirt on top of my jeans and close the door before everything falls out again, when a hand snakes out and slams it shut. I yank my fingers away just in time.

"Need a little help there, bro?"

A giant has found its way into the locker room.

A huge kid with the beginnings of facial hair smirks at me. His breath smells of pizza and Dr Pepper. I recognize him from math class. His name is Chance Sullivan, and he's on the basketball team. How could you name your kid "Chance" and ever expect him to be taken seriously?

He looms, serious enough. I start to swallow convulsively. There's not enough air in the room or spit in my mouth.

"How'd a third grader get in here?" he asks the room at large, and laughs. It is the noise of a frog burping. It's as dumb an insult as it sounds, and I have heard so much worse. *Huge-O. Tiny Tot. Lowrider. Smurfette. Bite-Size. Runt. Hobbit. Oompa Loompa. Arm Rest* was the worst because it invited physical contact. As bullies go, Chance is an amateur. For a second his words just hang there, and I pray it'll come to nothing. Then *one* kid who's sitting on the bench and tying his shoes chuckles. That's all it takes, *one* laugh, to make it legit. I want to crawl into my locker and hide under my sweatshirt.

"Whatever," I mumble.

"What's that?" Chance leans down and I shrink back, which is a mistake. Never retreat.

"Don't worry about it, bud." Chance pats me not-so-kindly on the shoulder. "You still got a few years for that voice to drop." His own voice is the rumble of a motor, a pack-a-day man, a superhero. I will not cry. I just hope I don't run. In the general allotment of "fight or flight," I only got flight.

Vij comes to my rescue. I am both thankful and irritated.

"Let's go," he says without looking at Chance.

"Vijay, my man. I was just introducing myself to your cousin." Chance is jolly now, like we're old pals. Of course he knows we're cousins. It's a small school. Everybody probably already knows my pants size too. Vij and I say nothing. Chance turns to go. I think it's over. Then he reaches out his sweaty hand and rubs my head. "For luck," he says. "Leprechauns are lucky, right?" So original. Call the tiny Irish kid a leprechaun.

I imagine myself saying something, fighting back: *Better a leprechaun than a troll* or *At least I remembered deodorant.* It could be the beginning of a new era. Hugo O'Connell saves himself and saves the day. No more "small" talk. I'd be funny and popular and living my *best* life. Finally one of the cool kids. But in the end, I just stand there, humiliation fizzing in my chest while everyone else files out. Vij puts his hand on my shoulder. I shake it off.

"Don't worry about it," he says when we're alone. "It's just 'cause you're new."

But we both know that's a lie.

Chapter Two

Fortune Favors the Bold

When I get home from school, the house smells like fried okra, which is another notch up the weirdness scale, because if our house ever smelled like anything back in Denver, it was takeout pizza or maybe burritos if Mom stopped by La Paz on her way home from work. My heart sinks. After a whole day of newness, I thought at least dinner would be normal.

I walk down the hall. It's white and bare and narrow. We haven't hung any pictures yet. But the tiny kitchen is an explosion of color, like it was helicoptered in from a rain forest in Brazil. The walls are white, but you can only tell in the evening when the sun can't shine through the green and red and yellow panes of the bay window. The colors shift constantly, like you're inside a kaleidoscope. The window looks out over the backyard we share with the people who rent the other half of our duplex, a couple who run the Italian place next to St. Stephen's Catholic Church.

Mom pokes her head out from behind a cabinet door. A square of yellow light flickers across her face, turning her blue eyes green. It's only four thirty, but her feet are already in the purple rabbit slippers I got her for Mother's Day. They were supposed to be a joke. I miss getting home first and knocking out an hour of solid TV watching before hearing the click of her heels down the hallway.

"Oh good. You're home! Do you remember where we put the big colander?"

"Ummm, what's a colander?" I dump my backpack on the floor, the only surface not covered in okra.

She shuts the cabinet and puts her thumbs to her temples, like it is all just *too much.*

"The *colander.* Come on, Hugo. The big metal thing with holes in it."

I spin in one slow circle. "Sorry, Mom, just not seeing it."

She sighs and lets her hands fall, then pulls a stack of cookbooks off a chair. "Sit. How was your day?"

She leans in too close.

"Don't look at me like that."

"Like what?"

"Like you're trying to read my brain waves."

"I'm not!"

She removes a baking sheet from another chair and pulls it up, too close again. Our knees touch. She's doing her therapist thing on me—studying my face, my posture; gazing deeply into my eyes so it becomes a staring contest. I lose every time.

"My day was as good as can be expected for a *first* day of *middle* school." Her mouth turns down at the ends. She has flour on her nose. I remember her note in my pocket and feel a flash of guilt. It's not her fault we're here. That prize goes to Dad. I add, "I have three classes with Vij," because more information, even the nonessential kind, is better than telling her about gym. *Third grade. Leprechaun.* My throat burns all over again. She can never, *ever* know that Chance exists. She worries enough as it is. I point to the cookbooks and the counters covered in pans and flour and what appears to be a small mountain of cornmeal near the toaster oven. "And how was *your* day?"

She sits back and looks around like she's just now clocked the mess. "I was trying to make your Grandma Sue's okra. I thought it would help." *Help what?* I want to ask. But Mom believes in total honesty, so I don't ask. I'm not sure I want to hear the answer. Mom's from Texas, but Colorado had mostly erased her Southern-ness. It only comes out when she's stressed. She smiles, but it looks like a struggle, which is the only reason I don't run from the room at what she says next.

"Will you do check-in if I promise to leave you alone after?"

I groan, as long and as loud as I can. "I hate check-in."

"Don't say you *hate* it. We have to focus on the positive, not the negative." She tugs at the hair just above my left ear that never lays flat.

"Fine. I don't hate it. But I seriously dislike it."

"Well, okay then." Pause. "But will you do it for me just this once on your very first day of middle school? Give me *one* adjective for the four categories. You don't have to explain. I just want four words, for your poor mother."

"Not cool. That's emotional blackmail. Therapists aren't allowed to do that."

"Fair play for moms, though."

She waits. She knows I'll do it. We've been doing check-ins since forever. When I was younger, I'd have nightmares and panic attacks every time I got sick and would have to go to the doctor. Which was all the time. I'd get ear infections and strep throat and rashes and cavities and every single fever and sometimes I'd have to ride in the ambulance. Mom says it's because I was born so early. Small size, smaller immune system, I guess. The check-in is to calm me down, make me feel "aware and in control of my emotions," as she likes to say. Try explaining *that* to your first-grade teacher when she asks you to join the rest of the class on the rug for circle time and you tell her you are not "emotionally ready for social interaction before nine a.m."

"Fine. One." I hold up a finger. "Mentally, I'm . . . fizzy." She opens her mouth. "No, you don't get to ask any more about it. Two." I hold up another finger. "Physically, I'm tired, duh. Three, emotionally—" I stop and think about it. New town. New school. New troll named Chance. No friends (cousins don't count). No Dad meeting me at the bus stop when I got home, like he promised. A mom who clearly didn't shower today and is now covered in corn-meal. "I'm . . . angry, I guess." I wait for her to say something about how I need to talk this out, but she doesn't. Two points for Mom.

"Spiritually?" she prompts, steering us along to the last of the four check-ins.

"Spiritually, I'm, um . . . I can't think of anything for that one. I am spiritually neutral right now. You think Sister Mary Margaret would make me stay late after Mass?"

She chuckles like I knew she would. Sister Mary Margaret is the nicest and oldest nun at our church back home. She smells like cinnamon and would forget my name five minutes after we said hello on the church steps. I kind of miss her.

"Well," Mom says, sitting back in her chair, "I guess that's pretty standard for a first day." She holds out a plate covered in shriveled bits of okra heaped on greasy paper towels. The shifting sun turns the plate red—a warning from the universe: DO NOT EAT! I take one anyway, because I am a good son. They're somehow burned *and* slimy at the same time.

"I really need to get back to work," she says with a sigh, sticking her finger into a piece of okra and squishing it like Play-Doh.

"You said it, not me."

I am half-kidding, but she doesn't laugh. She just stares at the plate with a blank look on her face. I shouldn't have said that. Mom loved her job. She loved helping people figure themselves out, and now she's here, wearing rabbit slippers and smushing okra. I want to apologize, but the words won't come. Sorry is much harder to say than to think.

We decide to eat out for dinner at the China Palace, which is so bad, it actually makes me wish for okra.

I bite into a nuggety chunk of sweet and sour chicken. Goo the color of Orange Crush squirts onto my plate. I draw scribbles in it with my chopsticks so I don't have to look at Mom who is looking at Dad who is looking at me over his glasses. I can *feel* them trading worried glances over their fried rice.

They want to know more about school. But what good would it do to give them the real picture? It's not like Dad's going to say, "Wow, son! I had no idea how hard it would be on you!" and whisk us back to Denver. His nose and cheeks are red from being outside all day at his new job. Must be nice. I disembowel an egg roll. We had better restaurants back home.

"It's only two and a half hours away," Dad had said when we drove off in a U-Haul full of all our worldly possessions. As if distance makes the difference when you're swapping out your whole life for another one. I miss my blue room and the glow-in-the-dark stars I stuck to the ceiling and the fact that I could walk to school so there was no need to deal with the bus, which Dad never apologized for not meeting me at this afternoon. I swing my legs in the booth. My feet don't touch the floor.

I was six the last time I was the new kid. Dad had signed me up for T-ball. I was so excited on my first day. I kept punching my new glove like they do in movies. The coach was mostly belly. Like, that's all you could ever look at—his big round stomach. I expected it to jiggle like Santa, but when I accidentally bumped into him it was hard as a rock. He looked at me like he didn't know what to do with me, like I was a dog that had wandered onto the field.

When it was time to start batting practice, Coach passed me a helmet. I hugged it to me carefully, like a bowl full of goldfish. But when I put it on, it slipped backward, right off my head and into the dirt. He checked the size and handed me another. Same thing. Again and again until the dugout was covered in upturned helmets like empty turtle shells. All the other kids were shoving one another and picking gum off the underside of the bench. They were ready to play.

Coach looked at me and the helmets and then walked ten paces onto the field, his stomach leading the way. He signaled to Dad, who was sitting with the other parents under the trees along the fence line. They had a conference midfield. I kept my eyes on them so I wouldn't have to look at my teammates. The coach's son, who played in an older league, started stacking up the helmets. He moved around me like I was a rock in the river.

The next week, before practice, Dad handed me my very own helmet. It looked exactly like all the others I had tried on. We were sitting in our old tan Jeep, but it was new then.

"Go on. Test it out, kiddo," Dad said, pushing his glasses up his nose, a nervous habit. I stuck it on my head like a total trusting dope. It fit like a dream. I took it off again to study it. It was magic. That's when I saw a long white strip of padding along the back.

"What's this?"

"Some extra support to make sure the helmet doesn't slip," Dad said, putting the helmet back on my head where it sat perfectly. It sounded totally reasonable to my six-year-old self. I wanted to play T-ball, and now I could. I ran onto the field without another thought—like a deer straight into the road.

The coach's son got to me first. "Peewee hat for the little guy, huh?" he said, and knocked his knuckles on my helmet. Then he pulled it off. When I made a grab for it, he held it above his head, and the little bit of white padding slipped out on the dirt between us. He burst into a high-pitched hyena laugh that went on forever. I can *still* hear it. The Pampers label stood out greener than the grass in the outfield. My dad had sent me to baseball practice with a diaper inside my helmet. I never played again.

I picture Chance in the locker room, rubbing my head "for luck," and my stomach rolls over on itself. What if this entire year is one long, miserable game of T-ball? I'm in the exact same humiliating situation and once again, it's all Dad's fault.

The waitress brings over our check and a plate of fortune cookies.

"You want to pick first?" Mom pushes the cookies toward me. She has long, graceful hands to fit her long, graceful self. Tonight, though, she looks tired. *Ditto, Mom. Ditto.*

I take a folded cookie.

They say you have to choose your own fortune or it

won't come true, like blowing out the candles on your birthday cake after making a wish. Dad picks the next one, and then Mom. We crack them open at the same time. My cookie's kind of bendy. Probably stale.

Dad nudges Mom. "You go first, Marion."

She flips over her slip of paper and then she snorts and reads, "A closed mouth gathers no feet."

"You're making that up." Dad grabs at it, but she holds it out of reach.

"I'm not!"

"What does that even mean?" I ask. I picture a colossal mouth sprouting hundreds of little feet along its upper lip, like a mustache.

"It means," she says, between bites of her cookie, "watch what you say so you don't stick your foot in your mouth."

Dad smirks and says, "Perfect for a therapist."

"Or *any* human," she shoots back.

I still don't get it.

Dad pulls the fortune from his cookie next. He laughs and thumps the table with his fist.

"The man on top of the mountain did not fall there."

He pops the entire cookie in his mouth. The crunching seems louder than humanly possible. "I like it," he says with his mouth full. "You have to work for what you want. Seize the day!" He's been spouting stuff like this since we moved. He's become an inspirational poster covered in kittens shouting, "Believe in yourself!"

It's this kind of thinking that landed us here in the first place. He quit his job as a computer engineer to be a ski instructor. Yeah, I know. Crazy.

One night he pulled into the driveway after another marathon workday and didn't get out of the car. He just sat there. For hours. Mom and I watched him for a while, but every time she went outside, he would hold up his hand like, "Give me a minute." At hour three, she ignored the hand and got in the Jeep. I started watching old reruns of *SpongeBob*.

When they finally came in, he took his tie off and dropped it on my head. "Here," he said. "Go run that through the garbage disposal, will you?" And we actually did, which was awesome. I wouldn't have done it, though, if I'd known it was going to shred our whole life.

Mom nudges my hand. "Your turn, Hugo."

I unfold my fortune.

"Now is the time to try something new," I read aloud. A moment of silence passes, and then Dad lets out a barking laugh. Mom and I just look at each other. All the worry about school comes up in a rush of partially digested chicken sludge. I swallow it down with my cookie.

Way to state the obvious, fortune gods.

Chapter Three

It's Science, I Swear

Dad missed dinner the last three nights. Mom asked Alexa to play Brad Paisley and tried to fry a chicken. He's gone again this morning before I leave for school. So much for the daily walks to the bus stop and the extra father-son "quality time" he said we'd be spending now that he didn't have to work every minute of the day.

"Something with the chairlifts, I think," Mom says when she hands me a PediaSure and I ask where he is. Her hair is a tangle, and I'm almost certain the bunny slippers have grafted to her feet. I stash the drink behind the coatrack when she turns back to the fridge. I still don't even know what he does exactly. Will he teach little kids to make the "pie wedge" shape with their skis? Will he operate the lift? Is he going to be the dude who stands there listening to '90s rock and holding the safety bar up for people? Is *that* what we did all this for? The night I shredded his tie felt important. We were teaming up to find a bigger and better life! But then we get here, and my world feels smaller than ever.

Outside, the lawn and streets glitter with a dusting of snow in the morning sun. I breathe in the cold, clean scent of it. My heart beats double time. Dad may be bailing on us, but the snow never does. It promises fresh powder and frozen ponds and road-sledding and, if I'm lucky, at least *one* day off school.

Vij was out sick last Friday, and it was the first time I'd been at Beech Creek without him. When Mrs. Jacobsen gave us twice the amount of homework for the weekend, I turned around already whisper-complaining to him because I forgot he wasn't there. Maddy, who sits across the aisle, saw it and laughed, and I wanted a sinkhole to open up and swallow me. And then in math, Mr. Wahl called on me to solve the equation on the board, and he let two solid minutes tick by without giving me any help while I tried to do it. Micah raised his hand and offered to jump in, but Mr. Wahl wasn't having it. My neck was so hot from all the eyes staring at me, it was the world's worst imaginary sunburn. At lunch I did the unthinkable—sat in Mrs. Jacobsen's room to eat so I wouldn't have to eat in the cafeteria because I'm still not sure if sitting with the newspaper crew is the right move and also, I didn't even know if they'd let me join them without Vij. I complain when he tries to help me out, because I'm already treated like a baby by Mom. I don't need my cousin to do it too. But without him there, it was like I wasn't there either. I wanted to blend in. Instead I felt like I'd been erased. That night I cried for the first time since we got here—feeling exactly like the baby everyone thinks I am.

But today, snow acts like a Band-Aid, covering all my grimy loneliness with a clean slate. I pass Jack and Gray in the hall before first period. They're throwing slap brace-lets against the lockers while two girls from history class huddle together in their short skirts and Uggs and ignore them. Everyone is easily distracted and hyper with the first snow. Except Emilia, of course, who sits cross-legged in front of her locker, typing away on her phone because heaven forbid she put it away for three minutes. Her sweat-shirt has a picture of a cougar on it, the school's mascot. Vij told me she's the only one who buys anything from the pep store. The newspaper staff meets for the first time today, and I still haven't given Vij a yes or no. No answer is an answer in its own way, right? I am about to risk a hello to Emilia when a wiry, dark-haired woman in a fleece jacket and pajama pants wanders down the hallway. She looks lost, but when she spots Emilia, she rushes right over.

"Hey, kid."

Emilia stands so fast it's like she's spring-loaded.

"*Mom*, what are you doing here?" she whispers, and I am frozen in place, the accidental eavesdropper.

"Funny story," her mom begins, and chuckles, but she looks frazzled and she's out of breath. Emilia crosses her arms. "I can't seem to find my phone and—"

"Again?"

"Yes, *again*," her mom says, "and your dad's working on a site today in Minturn. He's supposed to call when he's done so I can pick him up."

Emilia sighs. "Mom, your phone is plugged into the charger in the bathroom where you left it last night."

"Ahh. Forgot to check the bathroom." Her mom smacks herself on the forehead, like it's all a big joke. Emilia doesn't laugh. "And my work shoes?"

"I put them by the front door."

"Thanks, Em." Her mom tugs on Emilia's ponytail. "I'll see you after school."

Emilia sighs again. "No, Mom, you won't. I have the *Paw Print* meeting."

"Oh right, well, then after my shift at the restaurant."

As her mom leaves, Emilia huffs and yanks her ponytail tight again. It looks like it hurts.

"Uh, you okay?" I ask, because I have to pass right by her to get to my locker, and I can't think of a way to pretend I didn't see the whole thing. She startles and for a second forgets to ignore me.

"I'm *fine*. Why?"

"Uh, no reason."

Around us, kids scream and slip and slide on the floor that's wet from tracked-in snow. Everyone is happy. Everyone except Emilia. *And me,* I want to say. *I'm miserable too!* But that's not the kind of conversation you can have with someone who wishes you didn't exist. She turns her back to me, and I take that as my cue to shuffle to my locker.

On the way to algebra, a snowball whizzes between me and Vij and lands with a hard *sploosh* on the back of Micah's head. It splits and sinks down his collar. His shoulders shoot up to his ears and he turns, wide-eyed, to look behind us. From the farthest end of the hallway, Chance laughs like a tractor starting up. He's looking at me. That hit was a warning. I swallow hard. An icy cold settles over me that has nothing to do with the snow. My time of invisibility is up.

Vij yells, "Not cool, man!" but we only have thirty seconds before the bell, so I push Micah forward toward class. But he stops again and actually says "Good shot!" to Chance as Chance sprints by us into the room. I shake my head and run. Vij makes it in, then me. Micah stumbles in one second after the bell.

"Mr. Rosen, a word, please."

Mr. Wahl looms by the white board with the roll sheet in one hand and the green pad of detention slips in the other. He's in all black today, a suspicious crow.

"Mr. Wahl, it's not Micah's fault. Chance—" Vij begins, but Chance sits with his giant hands folded on his desk as if in prayer. The perfect student.

"I'm not talking to you, Mr. O'Connell."

"Yes, sir, Mr. Wahl?" Micah says. Water drips from his hair and makes a sad little puddle on the floor.

"Do you have the time?" Mr. Wahl inquires, polite and terrifying.

"Uh, what, sir?" Micah's hands are behind his back gripping the ends of his sleeves.

"Kindly share with us the time of day, Mr. Rosen."

We all watch as Micah turns a slow half circle to study the clock on the wall above the door. "Uh, it's 11:16, sir!" He sounds happy. Micah loves to get the right answer. He always does what's asked of him. He finishes his homework. He puts his lunch tray away. He even wipes down the table when we all get up. He doesn't deserve to be picked on by bullies like Chance or Mr. Wahl.

I want to say something. I want to rip the green pad from Mr. Wahl's hand and throw it out the window. I want to kick Chance's stupid size-thirteen feet. But I don't, because I'm scared of Wahl's beady stare *and* Chance's feet. After almost twelve years of drawing attention like a laser beam because of my smallness, I've learned to shrink back, literally, from the spotlight. But I hate myself for being scared, because Micah is standing there blinking and dripping and half smiling and seemingly oblivious to what's barreling toward him.

"As you are all aware"—Mr. Wahl turns to the entire class now—"class begins at 11:15." Chance smirks. Mr. Wahl continues. "Mr. Rosen, I'd like you to apologize to your peers for this unacceptable delay."

"We were basically late too, man," Vij says. I can't even nod.

"I was speaking to Mr. Rosen. But since it seems to be all for one and one for all, Mr. O'Connell, why don't you do the honors?" Wahl tears off three green slips and hands them to Vij. The entire class waits until Vij grits his teeth and hands one to me and one to Micah. I crumple the paper in my fist. My cheeks burn. I want to sit down. I want this to be over. But Mr. Wahl isn't done.

"Mr. Rosen."

Micah looks up from his green slip and stares at Wahl like he's lost the plot.

"Yes, sir?"

"We are still waiting for that apology."

"Oh! Uh," he faces the class, his eyes even wider than normal behind his glasses. Chance clears his throat and checks his wrist for the time on a watch that isn't there. "I'm sorry I was late," Micah squeaks out, ". . . and I'm sorry, for the, uh, delay!" he adds. He looks to Mr. Wahl, to see if that was okay, but Wahl is writing a series of complex equations on the white board. Apparently, the humiliation is over and now it's time to start class. "That will be one hour of after-school detention for the three of you," he says with his back to us. "Take your seats." And finally, *finally*, I slink down the aisle.

I once heard that crows are one of the smartest birds on the planet. They're as smart as your average seven-year-old. Which, as humans go, isn't that smart, but it's top-notch for a bird. They're like avian Einsteins. They also recognize human faces. Which means, if you get on the bad side of one of them, it will remember *forever*. Beyond forever, actually, because it passes on the grudge to its fellow crows and its crow babies. Without even trying, you've made an enemy for life. Mr. Wahl is a crow if I've ever seen one.

I never ever agreed to be part of the newspaper, and yet somehow I am in trouble with Emilia for missing the first meeting. Well, technically, since half the "staff" ended up in detention, there will be no first meeting today. Emilia is *not* happy about it.

She corners us by the cafeteria after the last bell rings.

"What were you thinking?"

"Don't blame us," Vij says. "Blame Chance."

"No, blame the Crow," I reply. At lunch I'd called Mr.

Wahl "the Crow" and Jack laughed so hard he spit a chunk of hamburger across the table. Gray high-fived me. For a second it felt like I was back in Denver with my old friends.

"*Technically*, I was the only one late," Micah explains. "These two tried to help." Emilia lifts her eyebrows at me and Vij, almost like she's impressed, even though I had nothing to do with it. I do not correct her. "Can someone let me borrow their phone?" Micah asks. "I have to call my granny!"

I hand him my phone, and when he turns away to dial, I mouth to Emilia, "His granny?"

"Micah's parents are divorced," she whispers. "His mom lives in Oregon, I think. He's usually with his dad, but when his dad got sent overseas, Micah moved in with his grandparents for a while."

"Overseas for what?"

"The army," she explains.

"His dad is in the military?" It's like trying to picture Micah with The Rock for a father.

Micah hands me back the phone, saying, "At least detention will give us time to finish our math homework!" Micah might actually be the nicest human on the planet. I want his dad to helicopter in and *crush* Mr. Wahl for what he did to him today. Micah deserves a hero. I clench my fists, more angry at myself than ever for not standing up for him.

The words come out before I can stop myself: "The Crow obviously needs a smoke and a girlfriend. Maybe then he'll shut up the next time somebody's *one* stupid second past the bell."

Emilia looks like I just spit in her Coke, but Vij busts out laughing.

"Dude!" he says, wiping his eyes like it's so funny he's crying from laughter. "How do you know he smokes?"

"Smoked. Past tense," I clarify, rubbing my hands together like a magician, because I haven't used this particular skill in ages. I explain: "When I turned in my equations, I saw an empty packet of nicotine gum in his trash. And an empty Red Bull and a supersize coffee cup. When people quit smoking, they drink a ton of caffeine to try to get the same kind of buzz."

No one is blinking. Maybe this was a mistake.

"You know all about the buzz, huh?" Emilia squints at me.

I learned the nicotine-caffeine thing from Mom. She would buy the double-caf coffee to make at her office for clients who couldn't go more than twenty minutes without a smoke break. But I don't tell Emilia that. Magic is better when you don't reveal all your tricks.

Vij shakes his head. "But what about the girlfriend? How do you know he doesn't have one?"

"Come on. You dress like that and breathe morning

coffee breath on everyone? There's no way he'd get a date, much less a girlfriend."

Emilia rolls her eyes. Micah tilts his head like he's still catching up. But Vij loves it.

"Well, that's just great. We're supposed to get the inaugural edition of the *Paw Print* out the first week in October, and you're busy getting detention and digging through people's trash," Emilia says.

"I wasn't *digging through* anyone's trash," I start to say, but she's pulling up her hood and walking toward the exit. I sigh, inwardly. One flash of brilliance and a few laughs and I'm already back to being invisible again. All I want is for Chance to ignore me and for my friends *not to*. Is that too much to ask?

"Uh, guys?" Micah asks softly. "Can you get detention for being late to detention?"

We sprint down the hall toward the library, squeaking our shoes extra loud because we can.

Detention, it turns out, isn't that bad. It's basically an hour of study hall, and the teacher on duty, Mr. Carpenter, my history teacher, doesn't even care if you talk as long as you're quiet and leave him alone.

After about ten minutes, Vij starts fidgeting, pulling the drawstrings of his jacket back and forth so they make a zzzzzing noise. The library is one big room, and it tends to echo. I grab his hand.

"So you *really* got all that about Mr. Wahl from his trash?" he whispers.

"Well, yeah." I pull out headphones to listen to music, even though I should be finishing my problem set for algebra. Micah, sitting on the other side of me, hums something that sounds suspiciously like "Elmo's World." He's already halfway through his math. He stops when Vij closes both our books and says, "Explain, Sherlock."

I think back to the day I first learned all the magical mysteries that trash could reveal. One afternoon, when I was nine, Mom tripped over the trash can in my room. A whole pile of Legos spilled out. I'd lost a wheel to the Batmobile and didn't want to play with them if it wasn't a complete set. She made me pick them all up and then handed me a bag so we could donate them to Goodwill. "Your trash says a lot about you, Hugo—what you value, what you think is worth saving and what's not. Think about that the next time you decide to throw away perfectly good toys," she said, and then sat on the floor with me and explained the science of garbage for the very first time.

"It's called garbology," I say now to Vij and Micah.

"What-ology?" Vij asks loud enough to make Mr. Carpenter clear his throat in a meaningful way without looking up.

"Garbology," I whisper, "is the study of people's trash to learn more about them."

Vij narrows his eyes.

"It's science, I swear!"

Micah nods. "Sounds cool to me."

"It's not just cool. It's a way to learn about a whole *society*." I'm in danger of revealing all my deep-seated nerdiness, the polar opposite of "cool," but between Vij and Micah, this is as safe a place as any. I keep going. "You can figure out what people value just by looking at their waste. Like, some cultures might throw away things that others would keep. I might toss a half-eaten apple, but somebody else would eat the whole thing, save the seeds, and grow a new tree."

"I tossed the Summer Scholars pamphlet my mom left on my desk this morning," Vij says. "That seems like a pretty obvious clue to my priorities."

"Yeah, we all know you are in an epic battle against your mom to prove your slacker status, but it's not always that obvious. Did you crumple the pamphlet?"

Vij scratches his head. "I don't remember."

"Because if you did, that would show more anger than if you just tossed it, still folded and unopened. Also, did you toss it on top or bury it?"

"I think I just threw it on top."

"Good. That means you're not trying to hide what you think about your mom's plans for you. You don't care if she knows you would rather die than go to summer school."

"Oh, she knows," Vij says as he sits back and gives me an unfamiliar look. It takes me a second to realize it's surprise and maybe a little awe. This might be the first time ever that I've managed to impress my cousin. I fight back a grin.

Micah sighs and begins to doodle a curling tree on the top of his math homework. "I wonder what my trash says about me?"

When Aunt Soniah picks us up, she gives me a quick kiss and asks Vij how newspaper went. He says it was great and we're working on a story about the new water bottle fill-up stations. He tells it so smoothly, I forget we weren't in Mrs. Jacobsen's room letting Emilia boss us around for the last hour.

They stay for dinner. Actually, Aunt Soniah brings dinner: Dad's favorite—meatball soup with extra meatballs. But Dad never shows and Uncle Dave's on a business trip, so it's just the moms and the cousins. While Mom hunts for bowls, I hear her tell Aunt Soniah, "His behavior is inexcusable. I'm not going to apologize for him. If he gets here in time, he can do it himself." I shrink back from the doorway. Mom would never say all that in front of me. Whenever I try to get one of them to side with me, they always say, "We're a team." Aunt Soniah clucks her tongue and doesn't ask more. That's how our family works. You deal with your drama on your own terms, but call if you need backup. By the time they come to the table with steaming bowls of meatball soup—"meatbowls" Vij calls them—they are both calm and smiling. I *knew* Mom was just as mad as I was about Dad never showing up when he says he will. I should be happy I'm right and Mom is on my side, but the victory feels empty.

Adra, Vij's eight-year-old little sister, sits next to me and chatters all through dinner about umlauts, the double dots you sometimes see over vowels, because her new best friend in third grade is named Zoë. Adra is all knees and elbows, and she wears glasses with the band around the back, like Micah. But the way she owns her nerdiness is most impressive. She's also already as tall as me.

"I have an announcement," Mom tells us after dinner over a round of Thin Mints from the freezer.

Aunt Soniah pauses in her sweep of invisible crumbs off the table into her palm.

Mom smiles at us. "I'm starting my practice back up."

"Of course you are," Aunt Soniah says with an approving nod. If she were in charge, she'd already have the name plate for the door: DR. MARION BARNES-O'CONNELL.

"Here's the catch. There's no affordable rental space. So"—Mom shoots me a look I can't read—"I'm going to practice right here."

"Here *where*?" I ask, spraying cookie crumbs all over the table. A few land on Vij's arm.

He rubs them off on my shoulder.

"Vijay!" Aunt Soniah shouts.

He smiles sweetly at his mother.

"Chew, then speak, Hugo," Mom says.

I swish some milk around in my mouth and then point at her. "Explain."

"I'm going to see clients right here at home. I'll start with couples counseling for now. Father Joseph at St. Stephen's says there're plenty of parishioners who could use it."

"I bet he did." Aunt Soniah snorts into her tea. From what Vij has said, Father Joseph is notorious for sharing other people's business. He's the worst gossip in the church.

"So these *clients* would be in our living room confessing all their secrets while we're, like, eating breakfast?"

"No, of course not, Hugo." Mom's starting to sound annoyed, like I'm ruining her plan by asking a simple and obvious question.

"I'd see them while you're at school."

"Well that sounds . . . weird," I say, because it does. Strangers in our house, using our bathroom and staring at our family pictures on the walls, if we ever get around to putting any up.

"I think that's smart," Aunt Soniah adds.

"It's something, at least." Mom crosses her arms. Does no one in this house care what *I* think?

While the moms keep talking, Vij, who's been quieter than normal all night, leans over and whispers, "I have an idea."

Chapter Four

The Garbologist

Vij won't tell me his idea until lunch on Monday.

"I'm waiting for the right audience," he explains before first period, and after second, and during third, when I ask him again.

Emilia hasn't forgiven us for forcing her to cancel the *Paw Print* meeting last week, but at least she's in a better mood now that Mrs. Jacobsen let her reschedule it for today. She actually puts her phone down and says hello when I get to the table at lunch. I've been here long enough now that I have a spot—facing the long windows with Vij on my left and Micah on my right. I am last to the table today and I can't lie, it's nice to see that little gap open and waiting for me.

I am folding a slice of pizza in half when Vij dumps a brown paper bag in front of me.

"I thought we agreed I would never brown-bag it again," I say through a mouthful of coldish cheese. It's not the *best* pizza in the world, but at least it's not heart shaped.

"We did, and I didn't." He points to his tray filled with three chocolate milks and a bag of Cool Ranch Doritos. His mom would kill him if she saw that. "This," he says, nudging the bag toward me, "is an experiment."

I set the pizza down and it unfolds slowly, like a tired butterfly. Jack leans over the table and tries to grab the bag. Micah gets to it first and helpfully holds it out to me. Even Emilia looks mildly curious in between bites of tofu nuggets.

"You know you want to, man," Vij says, taking the bag from Micah and slowly opening the top.

"No, I don't. I want to enjoy my cold pizza."

His smile holds all his old dares: jumping off the bridge over Cherry Creek, hiding out in the abandoned house by the gas station, sneaking out after dark to go night-sledding. I am equal parts terrified and excited, or maybe they're the same thing.

He tips the bag over so the contents spill across the table.

"Ummm," Gray says, picking up an eraser shaped like a strawberry. He sniffs it appreciatively. "Nice."

"I found a banana one!" Micah cheers and holds it out for Gray and Jack to smell, which they do. I stare at the pile and then back up at Vij's face and then back down at the pile that holds so much more than erasers.

"Vij, is this someone's trash?"

He nods and holds out his fist for a bump.

I shake my head. The garbology thing was a one-time deal. I already feel a little bad over what I said about Mr. Wahl, even if he is a crow. And if anyone else ever found out that the new kid *digs around in people's trash*, I'm done for. Vij is still holding out his fist.

"That's somebody's garbage? Get that away from my food." Emilia scoots to the far edge of her seat, dragging her lunch with her.

"Come on, Em," Vij says. "We all know tofu's not food."

"I'm not doing it, Vij," I say. "Where'd you get this anyway?"

"If I tell you, that's cheating." He lowers his fist and spreads the rest of the trash out so nothing overlaps. At least there's nothing actively rotting or crawling toward me in the pile. I try to remember all those dares and if I'd ever successfully said no.

"If I do it just this once"—I lean forward—"you have to promise this will be the only time."

"Oh, come on, what if—"

"I mean it, Vij. I'm not going to be the creepy kid in love with garbage." As if I didn't have enough bully-magnetism already.

"It's not creepy. It's cool!" Vij argues. He used "cool" in reference to me. It has its intended effect.

"Swear this is the only time."

I hold out my hand. He sighs and slaps it. "I swear. Now do your thing."

I stare at the mystery trash, trying to figure out where to start. My knees bounce under the table. Even if it's a terrible idea, I'm excited. Who doesn't love a good puzzle?

There are six fruit-shaped erasers—lemon, cherry, strawberry, banana, orange, and watermelon—the kind you'd get all together in a pack. I put them in their own little pile.

"Okay, this has to be from someone younger than us."

"Obviously," Gray says, even as he sneaks another sniff of the cherry one.

"It could be either a girl or a guy."

Emilia smirks from her far corner of the table. "Fruit *does* tend to be non-gender-specific."

"And?" Vij says, unimpressed.

I remember something Mom once told me about motives. You make different choices depending on what you value. It's why she makes our whole family write our top three priorities every year on January 1 instead of New Year's resolutions like normal people.

"It's not the *what* that matters. It's the *why*," I say, mostly to myself. Emilia picks up her phone, and Jack and Gray start fighting over a pack of Oreos. I'm already losing my audience.

"So, okay." I cup the erasers in my hand. "No kid would throw away perfectly good smelly erasers, right? There's either something wrong with the erasers or . . ." I look around at some of the other items on the table. My eye catches on a lined sheet of notebook paper. I pull it toward me. The word "syllabicate" is written out half a dozen times.

Jack squints at the paper. "What does syllabl . . . syllac . . . whatever mean?"

"It's the process of dividing a word into syllables," Emilia explains. So she *is* still listening. And also, *of course* she knows what that means.

"Right, so obviously this person is supersmart, or pretends to be," I say, and Emilia shoots me a look. "I think they threw away the fruit erasers because they were embarrassed of them. Maybe they thought they were silly?"

"And?" Vij says, still unimpressed. Garbology is both science and art. It's guesswork based on the information given. It's a *hypothesis*, not a diagnosis. What does he expect me to do, give him a name, weight, and eye color?

"And . . ." I study the rest: an empty tube of bubble gum toothpaste rolled all the way up into a tiny rectangle so that not a single squirt is left, a bunch of tissues (gross),

a neon orange Post-it Note with a pretty great drawing of a dragon on it that has been mostly scratched out. I pull the Post-it toward me. "And this person is picky about *everything*." I will not look at Emilia. I will not. I trace the six *syllabicates* in a row with my finger. "If it's not perfect or useful, it goes in the trash. So." I hold up my hand and count off: "Perfectionist. Diligent. Probably younger. Possibly artsy but doesn't pursue it. Values smarts above all else. And"—I pick up the erasers again—"needs to go play outside more."

Everyone is staring at me. Like *staring* staring. My stomach flips over. Did I overshoot and land all the way into the weird zone? "Or maybe it's just a kid who likes to doodle."

But Vij just spins the banana eraser on the table before saying, "Wow, my sister is a total nut-job."

"This is Adra's?"

That's some stressed-out garbage for an eight-year-old. I hope I'm wrong about what it means.

"So?" Vij turns to everyone else. "Creepy or cool?"

Micah and Jack and Gray all vote cool. Emilia shrugs. "Ninety percent cool. Ten percent creepy."

Vij shouts, "Hugo the Garbologist!" and a few heads turn. *Pleaseohpleaseohplease don't let this end up on Snapchat.* I want to slide bonelessly under the table.

"Vij, *no*. I told you, just this once," I whisper.

"Come *on*, Hugo!" He thumps me on the shoulder. "*This* is your superpower. You can look at a person's trash and see into their *soul*. How can you not want to use it?"

I've always wanted a superpower. Vij sees me wavering.

"We could find out tons of stuff about anyone we want!"

"And do what with it?" Emilia asks quietly.

"Yeah," I add because I want Emilia to forget the ten percent creepy and be on my side.

Vij rolls his eyes like this should be obvious. "This place is both totally boring *but also* full of people."

"So?"

"So, man, you could help us learn more about them." He stands up and puts his hand on his chest like he's saying the Pledge of Allegiance. "We can educate ourselves about our peers so as to better pursue empathy and inclusion." He absolutely rehearsed that at home.

Emilia tilts her head, considering. But I'm no fool. That's way too nice a motive for Vij.

"What do *you* get out of it?" I ask.

"Me?" Total innocent face. He pretends to pause and think about it. "I get to make this place a little more exciting."

"I think this place is plenty exciting!" Micah remarks. I agree. I just found a nice comfy spot midlevel in the social stratosphere. I don't want any attention drawn to me that might send me plummeting to the bottom.

This is basically Vij's way of passing the time that he can't spend on the mountain. He'll get to find out people's secrets and wishes and embarrassing quirks. He doesn't care about *empathy*. He wants reality TV. But if done correctly, and quietly and incognito, it *could* be used for good. I study Adra's scribbled-over dragon. What if I could drop hints that she should give the dictionary a break and take an art class? Wouldn't that be helping? What if I could do that for other people too?

I don't officially agree to anything, even though Vij begs. By the end of lunch, I find myself alone for a second, throwing away my half-eaten pizza in the big gray trash can as everybody races to class. Only then do I let myself think the other thing that I would never admit to anyone: I *did* feel a tiny bit cool after reading Adra's trash. It was the look on all their faces, even Emilia's. I had their attention and it wasn't for being small or the new kid. I was impressive for the first time in my life. How can I say no to that?

Chapter Five

The Doctor Will See You Now

Mrs. Jacobsen's room feels different after school—like walking into church on a Tuesday. Everything looks the same, but the vibe is off.

Mrs. Jacobsen, however, is exactly in character. Once we file in (I'm the last one), she fishes her glasses out of her hair and looks us over like melons she'd like to thump. Emilia isn't the only one upset that our first newspaper meeting was canceled.

"Right," she says finally after a long pause in which Emilia has already raised and lowered her hand three times. "Emilia is our editor-in-chief, as I'm sure you know. But because this is our first go-round with a newsletter, I think we need to establish the roles and responsibilities of everyone in the room."

"Wait," I say, before remembering to raise my hand.

Mrs. Jacobsen lets me go ahead anyway. "I thought this was a news*paper*."

"Well, you have been mis— or perhaps, underinformed. We will run our inaugural edition of the *Paw Print*, our news*letter*, the first week in October under Ms. Costa's initiative." She nods toward Emilia.

"You can't call it a newspaper unless it's longer than one page," Vij explains helpfully. Emilia glares at him.

"Not to worry, Hugo. We are off to a good start," Mrs. Jacobsen says with the same smile she gave me after handing back my first essay. Not very reassuring, as it was a C-. "Jack and Gray are our photographers."

Gray holds up a sleek digital camera. "Our parents got us these for our birthday this summer." Jack raises a separate lens and waves it around like a trophy. It's longer than my arm. I don't think I'd know how to use a camera that wasn't part of my phone.

"And Vij is our editorials writer and manager of the monthly calendar," Mrs. Jacobsen continues.

I raise my eyebrows at Vij. That seems like a thousand times more responsibility than he should ever be handed. He shrugs.

Micah turns a laptop toward me that shows blank white boxes with HEADER in big bold letters above them, and squished below those are a bunch of other boxes filled with the word "paragraph" over and over again in a tiny font. "It's a design template," he explains, which explains nothing at all. "I'm in charge of layout."

"And *I'm* in charge of all of you," Emilia says, oozing responsibility. She hands out the assignments for the day.

"What am I supposed to do?" I ask Mrs. Jacobsen, who is already retreating to her desk. She must have agreed to be the faculty advisor on the condition that she could stay in her room and do whatever English teachers do once the school day is over. Read Jane Austen? Play Scrabble?

"You help Vij write the editorials and do interviews," Emilia orders from the other side of the room.

"You can do whatever you'd like to do, Hugo. This is a *volunteer* position," Mrs. Jacobsen reminds Emilia and then asks me, "Do you ever read the newspaper at home?"

I read current events on my phone because we have to write about them for history class, but I don't think that's what she means. Does anybody actually read the news-paper anymore? The only part I like is the crossword. I've been doing the Saturday puzzle with my parents for as long as I can remember. Before I could even read, they'd let me cross off the clues after they'd completed them. I'm pretty decent now. Dad gets geography and sports. Mom takes science and literature. I focus solely on pop culture. There are a decent amount of DC and Marvel movie references these days.

All of this floats through my head, and by the time I realize I've been sitting here with my mouth half open without actually giving Mrs. Jacobsen an answer, she's already moved on.

"Why don't you follow Vij around on his assignment and have a think on it, and we'll go from there, hmm?" she says, waving us away.

I'm almost out the door when Emilia grabs me by the elbow. Her face is so close to mine, our noses almost touch. I take a slow, cautious step back, like you do with bears and other wild animals.

"Hugo, listen. I know you're only here because of Vij and I know Vij is only here because his mom made him and I know Jack and Gray are here because soccer season hasn't started and, well, I'm not sure why Micah is here, but I really, *really* need you to take this seriously, okay?"

"That was the longest, fastest sentence in history," I say.

"I'm serious."

"So am I. You clocked in at, like, three seconds. And the conjunctions!" She's only an inch or two taller than me. Our eyes are almost level. Almost.

"Hugo," she says.

"Emilia."

She sighs.

"Just don't screw it up, okay?"

With that resounding endorsement, I salute her. Then I remember her mom in the hallway in her pajama pants and Emilia's face stretched tight with embarrassment, and I add, "I promise."

Her shoulders lower half an inch, and she almost smiles. "You can call me Em."

"Okay, Em. I also solemnly swear to take the *Paw Print* seriously and to prevent Vij from doing as much harm as I am able. Okay?"

"Okay." Her grin is lightning fast—gone before I can fully register it. "Now get to work. We have deadlines."

I'm shocked to find Dad leaning against the Jeep outside the school when our meeting ends. This is the first time I've seen him in daylight in five days. It's colder than it was this morning. I shove my hands in my pockets and keep my head down as I walk to the car. Music blares from the stereo, and for a reason I can't pin down, it makes me mad. He waves a Starbucks cup under my nose when I reach him. It's my favorite—peppermint hot chocolate with extra whipped cream.

Something's up.

"Thought I'd take off early so we could grab pizza at Antonio's." That's our neighbors' restaurant, and he knows I love their pizza even more than I love this hot chocolate. I don't need to see Dad's trash to read the guilt on his face. He feels bad for ditching his family for the last few weeks, and he thinks pizza will fix everything. Some things never change. He used to do this back home when he'd work twelve-hour days, six days a week. I'd get home from school and he'd have the Jeep packed with all our camping equipment and he'd whisk us away and it would be awesome and we'd fish and sleep in hammocks under the stars and get lost in the woods for a day or two. But the minute we'd pull into the driveway, still smelling of campfire, he'd disappear, back to the office, and Mom and I would be forgotten, again.

I dump my backpack over the seat and slam the door. Heat blasts me in the face. It's aimed right at eye level, or, let's be clear here, *my* eye level, which is everybody else's middle. I tilt the vents. "Is Mom coming?" I ask.

"No. She's got a few phone consultations lined up. There's a lot to get ready before she can start seeing clients." He shrugs, like he doesn't understand how she'll be a therapist in our living room any better than I do. "So how was school?"

"Fine."

"What about the newspaper? Do you like the other kids?"

"News*letter*. And it's fine. They're fine." He'd know all about them if he were ever home.

After an awkward pause where he tries to take a sip of his too-hot latte and spits it back through the little hole in the lid, he says, "Well, work is fine too. Good, actually! They have me calibrating the lifts and clearing some of the trails. I get to drive a snowmobile!" His glasses fog up in the steam from his drink. I wonder what the other, *much younger* ski instructors with dreadlocks and goggle perma-tans think of my dad.

"That's great, Dad." I lean my head against the cold window and sip my hot chocolate. By the time we pull into Antonio's, he's asked me what I'm reading in English; told me all about his boss, a twenty-eight-year-old Swedish man who skied in the 2018 Winter Olympics; and wondered aloud if self-driving skimobiles could ever be a thing. He's trying to fit all the conversations he's missed into one. This is also what he does—he talks *at* me instead of *with* me. I sit a few seconds longer in the car after he gets out. I want a do-over. I want to rewind back to summer when we moved here, and I want him to keep all his promises. There have been too many missed dinners and missed meetings at the bus stop by now. It feels like we'll never catch up.

He waves at me from the open doorway to the restaurant. I leave my half-drunk hot chocolate in the cup holder and get out of the car. What choice do I have? What choice do I ever have but to follow him?

When our food arrives at the table, he eats four slices. I can't even finish one. I would have told him I had pizza for lunch, if he'd bothered to ask.

After spending all week trailing Vij while he interviewed the janitors and secretaries and student council members about the new water bottle fill-up stations, I've come to realize something: Vij could sell socks to an octopus. He can get anyone to go along with anything. "Are they hard to clean?" "Is the water any better than what's already in the fountains?" "Can we make it flavored?" "Can we get one installed in the locker room?" Everyone loves him and answers whatever he asks, even Janitor Phil, who thinks the only problem with Beech Creek Middle is that it allows children inside the building.

The thing about Vij is, if he really cares about something, no one can do it better. Like snowboarding. We'd all grown up doing the peewee ski school. It was twenty minutes on the mountain and an hour in the lodge drinking hot chocolate out of Styrofoam cups and comparing who had more mini marshmallows. "Skiing" was a moving sidewalk, like in the airport, that pulled you halfway up the easiest baby slope, and then you'd kind of scoot and skid your way down. The instructors would tell us to keep our skis in the shape of pie wedges or pizza slices to make sure we went slow. I always obeyed, because I had no choice. As the smallest kid whose mom sent him with a doctor's note listing all prior sicknesses and a novel on my traumatic birth, the instructors kept me right in front of them. Every time I almost fell, they would hoist me up under the armpits before I hit the ground. Sometimes I wonder if I'd be a different skier, a different kind of person maybe, if they'd let me crash.

But Vij never listened or waited for anyone to tell him what to do. He kept his skis parallel and shot straight down the mountain. Which is why, when we were eight and on a family trip to Copper Mountain, Uncle Dave let him snowboard. I think Uncle Dave figured it would slow him down. And it did, at first. Going down the mountain sideways instead of straight takes some getting used to. Vij ended up either on his back or his knees with snow up his nose most of the first day. But by the second, he'd started to get the hang of it, and by the third, my Aunt Soniah had to hide his snowboard during a bathroom break so he would stop and eat lunch. He was faster than I was on my skis. I didn't even ask my parents if I could try. I knew their answer.

Garbology is the first thing I can do that he can't. And now it's Friday, the weekend, and he hasn't brought it up *once* since Monday. Not even when Micah asked, "Will you look in Mrs. Jacobsen's trash and tell me if I passed my vocab quiz?" I almost do it. After trailing behind Vij on his interviews like a loyal sidekick, or lapdog, I miss that rush I got when I interpreted Adra's stuff and saw everyone's eyes get round and impressed. But I shake my head. It won't be as good without a bigger audience. And then I flinch at the thought. How did I go from avoiding it at all costs to wanting to make it *more* showy?

When Vij stops me by my locker after the last bell, I think for sure he's going to ask about it. I'm already preparing my agreement when he says, "My parents are bringing us over to your place tonight for fish Friday. Want me to bring the new Madden?"

"Uh, I guess." So he's already forgotten about garbology. It must not have been that impressive after all. I cough to cover the sound of disappointment in my voice.

"You *guess*? Where's the enthusiasm? Where's that old Hugo charm?" He dances around me backward as we move toward the parking lot. Two seventh-grade girls stop and watch. For a tiny second, I wish for him to trip. He holds out a fist for me to bump and doesn't miss a beat. When I get on my bus the seventh-grade girls are there too. They look right past me.

I keep my head down all the way home, regretting fish Friday and all the rest of Mom's new stress-induced Catholicism. It's just like the Southern cooking. She can't help herself. In Denver, Mom was too busy working full time to commit to all the rituals. But now we've done fish every Friday since we've moved. And by "we" I mean me and Mom while Dad is MIA up the mountain. We also never miss a Sunday Mass now, and I'm pretty sure Mom's got Father Joseph on speed dial. He lets her advertise her counseling services in the church atrium. She pinned up flyers on the notice board next to ads for roommates and pet sitting and cleaning services. Let me be clear: I do *not* want strange people crying on my couch, but if Mom going back to work gets me out of a few Friday dinners and Sunday morning Masses, I won't complain. I wish it would get me out of this one. For the first time since we moved, I don't want to hang out with Vij.

By the time the front door opens upstairs, I've managed to shove all my dirty clothes under the bed and all my clean clothes that Mom told me to fold a week ago into the back of my closet. Mom never cares what my room looks like unless we have company. I think people you're related to shouldn't count as company, but when has anyone ever asked my opinion? I sniff the air and cringe. I carried a tuna sandwich down here on Tuesday and just found it on my dresser. The air is heavy with fish funk.

"Hugo, dinner! Your cousins are here!" Mom yells from the top of the stairs, even though she always orders me to walk up the ten steps and talk in a normal voice.

Everyone's at the table when I get to the kitchen. Mom is dishing out shrimp scampi and laughing at Uncle Dave, who's telling some story about how he caught Aunt Soniah dancing to a Taylor Swift song.

"I was not."

"You were."

"I was reorganizing our tax files!"

"That was an awful lot of moving and shaking for tax purposes. It was"—he pauses and snaps his fingers—"what's that song? 'Baby, Just Say Yes'?"

Aunt Soniah moves Adra's juice glass closer to her with one hand and knocks Vij's elbows off the table with the other. She lifts her chin. "It was 'Love Story.'"

"Yes!" Uncle Dave hoots. It sounds just like Dad. They look alike too—tall, redheaded, and ten shades paler than the weathered Coloradoans. Mom didn't even set a plate for Dad. I guess we're done pretending he's "on his way." I glance toward the empty space where he should be. I would trade a million special dinners at Antonio's for him to show up at the kitchen table.

"Adra, honey, how's school?" Mom asks.

Adra puts down her fork and dabs her mouth with her napkin like a dainty old lady. "It's going well, Aunt Marion. Thank you for asking." I want to ask about her drawing. I want to buy her a new pack of erasers. I want her to stop cutting each shrimp into three equal parts before eating it.

"And you, Hugo?" Uncle Dave turns to me. "Vijay told me you joined the newsletter with him. Excellent!" Uncle Dave reminds of a puppy that always lunges with good-natured friendliness at the nearest human. I guess that's why he's in sales.

"Uh, yeah. I'm still trying to figure out what I'm supposed to be doing, but it's good so far."

"But you're settling in okay?" Aunt Soniah asks. Her eyes dart toward Mom, who shakes her head a fraction. What was *that* about?

Vij answers for me. "Hugo's great, Mom. Can we go downstairs now?" He doesn't check with *me* if I want to go downstairs. Typical. It's Vij's world and we're just living in it.

"Not until you're done eating."

He shoves a giant forkful of pasta into his mouth, chews, coughs, drinks his entire glass of water in one go.

"Done!" His chin is shiny with butter.

"Disgusting," Adra says.

"Agreed," Uncle Dave adds.

Vij grabs me by the elbow and pulls me toward the steps before anyone, including me, can disagree.

We're one hour into Madden and his Aaron Rodgers has beat my Cam Newton three games in a row. And he's not even trying. He keeps checking his phone.

I miss another first down and Vij doesn't notice. I throw the controller across the room. That finally gets his attention. He looks up from his phone, but keeps his finger on it so it stays lit.

"Dude, what was that?"

"I hate Madden."

"Nobody hates Madden."

"Don't tell me what I hate."

He raises his hands. The problem with cousins is you can't fight with them like you fight with friends because you can't escape them. They will always be there at the fish Friday or Christmas dinner or summer cookout. You're stuck for life.

I could explain to Vij why I'm mad—but then I would have to admit that I really wanted to do the garbology thing, and that is just too embarrassing, even for family. Instead, I sigh and retrieve the controller from under my desk.

"Let's just play," I say. But before I can unpause, the doorbell rings. It's nine o'clock. Nobody rings the doorbell this late, unless Mom finally got fed up with Dad and locked him out.

You can hear every tiny noise from down here, whether you want to or not. Chairs scrape back from the table. Footsteps plod down the hall. The door creaks open and voices start talking in muffled tones. Finally, the sound of Mom calling down the stairs, "Hugo, honey, can you come up? You have company."

Company? Everyone I know is in this house. Out of the corner of my eye I catch Vij smiling, smirking really. He's not looking at his phone anymore.

"Who did you invite over?"

"No one." He shrugs and pulls at the hood of his sweatshirt. "I mean, I might have mentioned to a few guys that we were hanging out tonight."

"What guys?"

"Just Jack and Gray and Andrew and Micah, but Micah

couldn't make it. His grandparents don't like to drive at night."

"Andrew? I don't even *know* Andrew. Isn't he friends with Chance?" My pulse ramps up. Mom shouts my name again.

"Andrew hangs around Chance because he wants to get on the basketball team, but he's not really friends with him," Vij explains, calm as can be. "He's a good guy. I swear."

Maybe it's true, but I don't want to risk Andrew reporting back to Chance about my Star Wars bedspread. My fishy basement bedroom. The clothes spilling out of my closet. You don't give the enemy a tour of your headquarters.

"Hugo, get up here now!" Mom is on the top step. I can see her shadow. I can't move.

"Who said you could invite *anyone* over? This isn't *your* house," I whisper to Vij.

Vij stands and pulls me up with him. "I'm doing you a *favor*, man."

I knuckle-punch him hard in the shoulder and walk upstairs.

Jack and Gray and Andrew are huddled in the hallway, which still doesn't have any pictures on the walls and looks even smaller with all three of them trying to stand on the rug where Mom has asked them to take off their boots.

"I'll bring down hot chocolate in a little bit. Or Dr Pepper? Would you boys like some Dr Pepper? We also have some fudge that Sister Anita gave us last week. Oh wait"—she throws up her hands like a crossing guard—"is anyone allergic to nuts?" I can't find a single word and Mom's got a million too many.

"Hey, guys!" Vij calls from behind me. "Come on down! We've got Madden."

Andrew gives me the cool-guy nod as he marches past. When he's gone, I turn to Mom.

"I've got it. Stay. Up. Here."

"All right." Her voice goes high. "You boys have fun!"

Once we're downstairs, I don't know what to do. I only have two controllers, so Madden's no good unless three people want to watch, and there's nothing less exciting than watching someone else play a video game. Jack throws himself face-first on my bed and Gray dumps both their backpacks on the floor. Andrew's in my history class, but we've never actually talked. He's tall, like five and a half feet, and he looks exactly like every basketball player in existence—knobby shoulders and giant hands. I watch him turn in a circle, checking out my room. It's like watching the security guard go through your stuff at the airport. You know there's nothing to hide, but still, you feel guilty.

"What's that smell?" he asks.

"Uh, my mom made fish."

"Oh. Cool." He wipes his nose on the sleeve of his

sweatshirt and hands me his backpack. I hold it, because, what does he want me to do? Hang it up like a coat? He watches from his great height. No one speaks.

Finally, Andrew scratches at the too-long hair by his collar and asks, "So how does it work? Do I show it to you all at once or one thing at a time?"

"Uh? What?"

I turn to give Vij the "this guy is crazy" look, but Vij is smiling that stupid smile and suddenly it all clicks.

"No." I toss the bag back to Andrew.

"What?" Vij is the picture of innocence.

"I'm not doing it." Now that garbology is back on the table, I panic. Just because Vij and the guys and Em thought it was awesome doesn't mean someone like Andrew will. And he will *for sure* go back and tell Chance what a loser I am.

"Look, Hugo," Gray says, squatting down next to his backpack, "I know you still feel weird about looking through people's trash."

I feel my ears go red, because that's not actually true. I'm worried about how people will react, but the actual act of garbology, I love. It's like having access to a person's diary and all their secrets, whether they mean to share them or not.

"So you all planned this?" I ask Vij. I am equal parts relieved that he didn't forget and terrified about what will happen next if I agree.

Andrew turns to Vij.

"He didn't know I was coming? Is this garbology thing even real?"

"Of course it's real!" I snap, because he can at least talk to *me* in my own *room*.

"Hugo," Jack says, "Andrew here has a problem and we think you might be able to help."

"What's his problem?" I say to Jack because I'm not ready to talk to Andrew again.

"Uh-uh," Vij says, stepping forward. "You have to look at what he brought first and *then* we'll tell you. We don't want to skew the results."

I look from Vij to Jack to Gray, who is holding his ginormous camera, and finally to Andrew. They are all staring expectantly, waiting for me, Hugo the Garbologist, to do my thing. Something like pride swells in my chest and overrides the fear. Forget Chance. Tonight, I can do the one thing I know better than anyone else in the room.

"Fine," I say, pretending to be reluctant, but when Andrew passes me his bag again and grins, I can't help but grin back. "But no pictures," I add.

"Come on!" Gray protests.

"No pictures or no garbage."

"Okay! Okay!" he says, and stuffs the camera into his backpack.

I unzip Andrew's pack slowly, not knowing what will

spill out, but it's all contained in a plastic trash bag. I pull it out gently.

"Okay, everybody sit," I say, and they do. It feels good to be in charge. Nobody ever listens to me, especially not guys like Andrew. Definitely not Vij. We circle the bag like it's a Ouija board but lean waaaaaay back when I untie it and the smell of feet and onions comes wafting into the room.

Like he's assisting with a surgery, Vij hands me a hanger from the floor, and I use it to poke around in the bag for a minute. All eyes are on me, so I make sure to do it slowly and with much ceremony. The contents of Andrew's trash are as follows:

- Three empty 20 oz. Diet Mountain Dews and
      one half full of brown liquid
- White tape twisted up in a ball
- A bunch of tissues that I don't even want to
      touch with the hanger
- One ten-dollar lotto card with all the spaces
      scratched off
- A handful of chewed sunflower seeds,
      barbecue flavor
- Three Band-Aids, which I also don't touch with
      the hanger
- One empty Vanilla SlimFast

I sit back on my heels and think. Everybody watches me. Maybe Sherlock Holmes wore a hat to avoid eye contact.

I shake the Mountain Dew bottle, but I don't have to open it to guess the brown liquid.

The white tape is the athletic kind you'd use on a knee or elbow.

The barbecue sunflower seeds are my favorite flavor, but since this is not my trash, I don't think that helps.

I rub my head. I have no idea whose trash this is. None. What if I can't do it? What if I guess wrong, and then not only will Andrew *not* be on my side, but he'll also tell people I am a teeny, tiny faker?

My foot brushes up against the trash bag. It looks familiar.

"Well?" Andrew says, bouncing his knees up and down in anticipation.

I have one guess. It's a shot in the dark and based more on Andrew than the trash itself, but I'm not going to tell him that. If I'm wrong, then I will quit Beech Creek and homeschool myself in the basement while Mom tells couples how to make marriage work (hah!) upstairs.

"This is Coach Anderson's." I don't ask it. I say it. Always sound sure.

"Yes!" Andrew cheers. "That is so awesome."

I let out a breath. I feel like I just passed a very important quiz.

"Told you," Vij says to Andrew as Jack high-fives Gray. All my earlier anger at Vij evaporates. He's the reason four guys are sitting in my room on a Friday night.

"So how'd you guess?" Andrew asks as we all look back down at the trash like it's treasure.

"It was the bag," I say, then pause for suspense. "They only use these really thin ones at schools and, like, the mall. But this one's too small for the mall trash cans." Nobody seems to wonder how I know what mall trash bags look like. Last month I accidentally threw away my phone with my Taco Bell wrappers at the Avon shopping center and had to dig it out. An unfortunate incident now turned lucky.

"But how'd you know it was Coach Anderson's?" Gray asks.

"Well, consider the tape and the sunflower seeds." I cross my arms, sitting back a bit like Mrs. Jacobsen when she explains something to the class. "I've seen him tape his knee after gym. And also, he always smells like barbecue."

"He *does*, doesn't he?" Jack says, totally amazed.

I poke the Mountain Dew bottle with the hanger.

"I didn't know he dipped, though."

Andrew nudges the bottle with his foot and the murky liquid sloshes around. "Gross. You sure that's what that is?"

I nod. I had a babysitter back in Denver who played

high school baseball. He'd take me to the park and sit on a swing and spit the exact same color and consistency into an empty Dr Pepper can. Wintergreen was his preferred flavor of chewing tobacco. Mom fired him when she caught me storing my matchbox cars in his empty Skoal container.

I pick up the bottle and hold it out to Andrew. "Why don't you take a sip and see?"

Everybody scurries back.

"Nah, man. I trust you."

Just like Mom does with her clients, I'm establishing credibility. They have to think I'm the expert if they're going to listen to me.

"So why'd you want me to look at his trash, anyway?"

Andrew leans forward and clasps his huge hands together like he's about to pray. "I *really* want to make the team this year."

I shoot Vij a look. He shrugs in response. We're both thinking the same thing. How is Coach's trash going to get Andrew on the team?

He's still talking. ". . . and I didn't make it last year because even though I was the tallest on the elementary team, I wasn't as coordinated or whatever. I need to know everything I can about him, to, you know, get on his good side. And I thought you could tell me?"

"Umm," I mutter. Andrew looks so desperate, like he

might actually cry if he doesn't get on the team, but this could be beyond my skill level. What if I get it wrong, and then I'm the reason he doesn't make it?

"Let's see what I can do for you," I say as confidently as possible while swallowing a whole mouthful of fear.

"Cool, man, thanks!"

We all gaze down at the pile. I think about the "why" not the "what," like Mom taught me. Why all the sunflower seeds? Why the SlimFast? Why *so much* tape? There's always a chance part of this could be someone else's. It's not guaranteed that just because it's beneath his desk, it belongs to him.

I stare until the whole mess blurs. Then, like a puzzle, the pieces start to slip into place, almost without me trying. I wait while they rearrange themselves in my brain. After a long time, I look up. Everyone's watching me again, but I'm not nervous now. Maybe it's because I know Andrew's not going to make fun of me. Or maybe it's because I'm pretty sure I'm right.

I point to the tape. "His knee's been bothering him more. That explains why he's going through so much tape. It also explains the sunflower seeds and the Slim-Fast."

"How?" Vij asks.

I pause for a beat to build suspense.

"He's trying to lose weight to take some of the pressure

off his knee," I explain. "The sunflower seeds are the only healthy thing in the snack machine. After that it's Snickers and Funyuns. And the SlimFast, well, have you ever seen the cafeteria put out a 'lite' menu?"

Vij should have made the knee-weight connection. Uncle Dave just told us tonight at dinner about a guy in his office who had to go on a diet because his doctor warned it was either that or he'd be replacing both knees sooner rather than later. Old sports injuries in old, overweight guys is nothing new.

"If you want him to notice you," I say to Andrew, "maybe tell him he looks like he lost weight. Or ask him about his knee or something. Start a conversation."

He nods and then nods again as he processes it. "Yeah, yeah. I'll do that. That's great, thanks!" And then, I'm not even kidding, he reaches out to shake my hand. So this is what respect feels like.

"Jackson? Grayson? Your parents are here!" Mom calls from the stairs. We scramble to shove everything back into the bag before she sees. Let her think we're burning brain cells playing video games. It's better than sifting through somebody else's trash. The twins' parents are giving Andrew a ride, so he gets up too.

While everyone's pulling on their shoes, Mom whispers, "Did you have a good time?" I give her a quick undercover thumbs-up and then nudge her toward the living room before she can invite them all back for a sleepover.

I hold up my hands for a round of high-fives as everyone, including Vij, shuffles out the door. And then, when they're gone, I lean against it, weak with relief and the sweet taste of victory.

Chapter Six

....

Winter Wonderland

I smell it even in my underground room—colder, sharper air that can mean only one thing: big snow.

When I pad upstairs in my socks, Mom and Dad are standing by the front window looking out over the street. They're both still in their bathrobes, Mom leaning into the crook of Dad's arm.

Snow sits piled up on the windowsill, and ice spiderwebs across the panes of glass. It looks too perfect to be real, like spray snow from Target, like Mom and Dad all happy after weeks of barely talking and angry whispers when they think I can't hear. But I'm still riding my own wave of happiness from my epic garbology session with the guys last weekend, so I'll take it. I lean against the window beside Mom.

Dad grins and runs a hand through his crazy hair.

"We never got *this* kind of snow back home until, what, November?"

"That's what happens when you move four thousand feet higher," I say. "You get four thousand more feet of snow."

"I bet it's eighty degrees in Texas," Mom laughs. She's probably right. I remember running around in shorts and flip-flops during Christmases at my grandparents' house. We watch a car crawl by on the all-white street. It fishtails a little at the four-way stop. They haven't switched to their snow tires yet. No one expected this much snow this fast.

"Come on, kid," Mom says, pulling her robe tighter. "We'll need to dig out your down jacket if you're going to take the bus." Nothing cancels school out here. Not even big snow.

Dad walks me to the bus stop on his way to work. He whistles off-key. I want to stay mad at him for being gone so much, but it's like fighting a smile—not worth the trouble, and kind of impossible anyway. Instead, I squint in the glare of the sun off the snow and slow my walk to match his. For once, we're not in a hurry. When the bus arrives and the doors open with a whoosh of heat, he tugs on the back of my hood.

"I'll pick you up after school today"—he pauses—"if that's all right?"

Dad's never asked my permission for anything before. It's as unexpected as the weather.

"Uh, okay."

"Good." He claps his hands together and blows into them. "Because I've got a surprise."

When I get to school, there is a snowman in the hallway outside the band room. An actual snowman. With a pink fleece hat and carrot nose and two pine branches for arms. A crowd of seventh graders are taking pictures of it with their phones. I hope they click fast. Janitor Phil approaches with his mop and bucket at full speed, and Principal Myer is on the intercom threatening everyone with detention if they don't hurry to class. Poor Myer. She should know better. School might not be canceled, but there will be absolutely no learning today.

In English, Mrs. Jacobsen smiles at me when she hands back my essay, and I can't tell if it's a good-grade smile or a bless-his-heart, pity smile. It's a B+. I shoot her a happy-with-my-grade grin, and Vij leans over my shoulder.

"Not bad."

"What'd you get?"

He holds it up. A, of course. I fist bump him. With the snow and an actual promise from Dad that I'll see him after school, I'm feeling generous. I'm in such a good mood that when I walk into algebra, I don't notice that everyone is standing around Mr. Wahl's desk and laughing until I get to my seat. "What are they all looking at?" I ask Vij, who is already at his desk. He won't meet my eye and he's never early. Ever.

Right then, Mr. Wahl marches in with a stack of calculators, and everyone scatters. I see what's on the desk at exactly the same time as the Crow: a twelve-pack of nicotine gum topped with a big red bow. I can feel Vij holding back a snicker from behind me, and my good cheer vanishes in a puff of fear and foreboding.

Mr. Wahl freezes. The clock ticks. Somewhere in the room, someone coughs to cover a laugh. He drops the calculators onto his desk with a clatter. It's the loudest sound in the universe.

He turns to the room. "Who?"

Nobody moves. Nobody even blinks. I might throw up. Hot acid crawls up my throat. This is all my fault. I sink in my seat, and Mr. Wahl catches the movement. His head tilts toward me.

From behind me, Vij whispers, "Don't. Move."

Sweat drips down my collar. The heaters are working overtime. I feel sick and sticky. This is all garbology's fault, or mine really, because didn't I know what Vij would do if he found out about it?

"Mr. O'Connell. No, not you," he says when I open my

mouth. "Mr. *Vijay* O'Connell. Do you have something you'd like to share with the rest of the class?"

Behind me, Vij leans back in his chair. "Well, I was just wondering, sir . . ." He points to the Crow's desk with his pencil. "How did you get so lucky to get a secret Santa in October?"

Chance snorts from the other side of the room, which makes a couple of other guys laugh, which makes a few of the girls giggle, and Mr. Wahl's face gets redder and redder. But he doesn't speak. Pretty soon the laughs are smothered by his terrifying quiet. He turns and folds his hands behind his back. "Open your books to the problem sets," he says in a monotone. "You have until the end of class to complete chapters twelve through fifteen."

Micah, who sits in the front and is wearing a cranberry red turtleneck, raises his hand. *Danger! Danger!* I want to shout, but of course I don't, because I'm too much of a chicken.

"Yes, Mr. Rosen?"

"Sorry, sir, but—" Micah pauses, swallowing hard. "We haven't started chapter fifteen yet!"

The Crow pivots slowly toward him. "Is that a problem, Mr. Rosen?"

"Uh, no, sir. I'm sure I can piece it together!" Micah's ears disappear into his turtleneck.

"Good. Now begin."

Everyone gets busy opening their books and pulling out notebook paper. I'm the only one who sees the Crow swipe the whole packet of gum, red bow and all, off his desk and into the trash.

After class, I steer Vij toward the lockers next to the cafeteria. Thanks to him, the Crow is going to push the whole class harder and harder until there's no one left passing, except Vij, the genius. Vij will always pass. This will never touch him.

Before I can get us to the lockers, an eighth-grade girl from the soccer team puts a hand on my shoulder. Her name is Jasmine, and she is taller than me by at least a foot. She is also the first girl to touch me since I moved here. All thoughts of retaliation evaporate. I let go of Vij.

She looks down at me and smiles.

"You're Hugo, right?" she asks.

"Umm, yeah?" My voice goes high. The beads on the ends of her braids are the school colors: blue and yellow. I stand up as straight as I can.

"So, uh . . ." Her voice trails off. She holds out a plastic Walmart bag. We both stare at it like we're not sure how it got there. "You're the guy who reads people's trash?" She glances over her shoulder like she's afraid we're being watched.

Vaguely, like a distant memory, I recall something

bad happening in math class last period regarding gar-bology. But all warning bells of danger are overridden when Jasmine leans in to whisper, "I mean, if you looked in this bag you could, like, tell me about the person who threw this stuff away, right?" She smells like strawberry ChapStick, and I find myself nodding and nodding and nodding until I have to will my head to stop.

"That's right," I say, my voice cracking on "right." Behind me, Vij starts to laugh, and I step back so that I land not so gently on his toe. "Ask me anything," I say.

Jasmine grins at me—not Vij, *me*. I smile back.

"Okay, so, this is Thomas Findley's trash. You know him, right? He's, like, the captain of the soccer team, and he's got light brown hair, more like caramel-colored really, and these *deep* green eyes and—"

"Yeah, we know who he is," I interrupt. It's getting harder to smile.

"Okay, well, umm, I guess I just kind of want to know more about him, you know? More than, like, how tall he is, which is *so* tall. Can you tell me, you know, what he's into?"

Jasmine holds out the bag.

I don't want it now. I don't care what Thomas Findley, star soccer player, is into. Is this how fortune-tellers feel? People don't come for the truth. They come to get their wishes granted. They want you to tell them what they want to hear. But . . . Jasmine didn't know my name until today. She didn't even know I *existed*. You take what you can get, I guess. I open the bag.

"Where did you get this?" I ask as we all peer into it. Jasmine twists one of her braids around her finger.

"Umm, well, we had a group study session for history at his house, and I thought . . ." She trails off again. "I mean, it's just trash, right? He's not going to miss it."

"Uh, right." I do my best to ignore the creepy image of Jasmine digging through some guy's trash while his back is turned and focus instead on the contents:

- Two broken pens with the caps chewed
- A crumpled piece of graph paper with a sketch
     of a mountain that looks like something
     you'd build in Minecraft
- A broken hair tie
- Two sheets from a vocab quiz separated and
     folded in half
- Three pizza crusts and two empty packets of
     red pepper flakes from Papa John's

That's it. Not much to go on. Jasmine holds her breath. "Well?" Vij prompts.

"Ummm, the sketch is cool. Have you seen him draw before?"

Jasmine starts to shake her head no, pauses, and

begins to nod rapidly. "Yes! He's always bent over his notebook in history. I thought he was taking notes, but he's actually terrible with the timelines. This makes much more sense! So he's an artist," she says dreamily, and I try not to gag.

"Also, uh, he might be in learning services, for, uh, English, so maybe don't compare grades?" *Or remark on his bad timelines in history,* I think.

"I would *never*," she says, and puts her hand on her heart.

"He seems to like spicy food though, so next time you're around him, you could talk about your favorite Indian or Mexican restaurant or the hot wings in the cafeteria?" I'm kind of shooting in the dark here—trash I can handle, but dating advice? Not so much. Jasmine doesn't seem to notice.

"Yes, perfect!"

"Does he have a girlfriend, though? Or maybe a little sister?" I ask.

"Oh, you mean the hair tie?" Jasmine says. "It's his. Did I mention his long hair? He likes to put it up during games." She zones out for a second—probably picturing Thomas's long, flowing hair. I clear my throat, and she snaps out of it.

"Hugo, thank you. *Really*. This was amazing. Totally," she says, and takes back the bag. And then she gives me a quick hug. I watch her walk toward the cafeteria while every single atom in my body zings. Garbology is a beautiful thing.

"How'd you know about the English stuff?" Vij asks once she's out of earshot.

Thomas's vocab quiz was separated out into single pages instead of stapled and double-sided, like normal. When you have extended time to finish, the teacher only gives you one sheet at a time. Cole, back home, had the same setup last year. But I'm not telling Vij any of that because I just remembered that I want to pummel him.

I shove Vij toward the cafeteria. Today they're serving potato salad, tuna salad, chicken salad, and watermelon. Picnic food on the snowiest day of the year. We collect our food in silence, but as we get closer to our table, I can't take it anymore. "What you pulled in math class was *not* cool! And I thought we swore the garbology stuff would stay a secret. How did Jasmine even find out?"

"Who says it was me who told?" Vij sets his tray next to mine and begins to pick seeds out of his watermelon.

"Come on! Of *course* it was you! You've managed to tell the whole school I'm the trash-whisperer!"

"And you just had the longest conversation with a girl you've ever had in your life, so don't whine about it!" Vij says, waving his plastic fork in my face.

I grab his fork and then don't know what to do with it.

I clutch it, like a spear. Farther down the table, Em and Micah watch us whisper-yell. I'm glad the twins aren't here to see this.

"I single-handedly made you cool and all you do is complain."

"*You* made me cool?" I snort. "What are you, king of the school?"

"No. I never said that." He folds his hands together on the table. A super-annoying picture of calm. "But you have to admit, what happened back there with Jasmine, you *liked* it. You liked the attention, and you liked being right."

Em raises her eyebrows.

Of course I did. I can still feel the tingle in my arms from her hug and how she paid attention to me for something other than my size. I can't say he's wrong. But I'm also *never* going to say he's right.

"*You* didn't make me cool. Garbology made me cool. And since I'm the only one with that skill set, do the math . . . *I* made me cool." I catch Em shaking her head out of the corner of my eye, but I don't even care. Let her judge me. I'm just speaking the truth. "*You're* the one who almost ruined it all with your gum stunt in math."

"Come on, Hugo," he says. "We both know that if it weren't for me, you'd still be shuffling through the halls feeling sorry for yourself."

I slam his fork down. "Well I guess I should say 'thank

you,' then. For making me *cool* right before you get me *expelled*. Everyone is going to blame *me* for what happened in Mr. Wahl's class!"

Vij picks his fork up, and through a huge bite of potato salad, he says "They'd have to learn your name first, cuz."

His words squeeze my heart like a fist—a fist that wants to punch back. I shove my tray. It bangs into his with a deafening clatter. They fly off the table and land on the floor in a wet mayonnaise-y, watermelon-y heap. The room goes deathly silent, and all heads turn toward us like we're in some zombie movie. One of the cafeteria workers begins to walk over. Em scoots as far away from us as she can get without actually switching tables. Micah, though, gets down on his hands and knees and begins to swipe at the mess with his one and only paper napkin.

Before I can decide whether to hide or help, Janitor Phil materializes out of nowhere and lays heavy hands on my and Vij's shoulders. "You better clean every bit of this up," he growls, "or you'll be spending the afternoon with me, scraping scuff marks off the gym floor." He's got a bristly beard and smells like bleach—all signs point to "do not mess with me." We nod.

He tosses us a roll of brown paper towels, the kind that don't soak up anything. We begin to shovel and scoop the lumps of chicken and potato and other goo back onto our trays. We do not make eye contact. Janitor Phil watches with his arms folded. He doesn't move until we've wiped the floor clean with water and patted it dry. Micah and Em watch from the sidelines as teachers order everyone else to class.

After the floor is better than we found it, Janitor Phil dismisses us to gym—from one nightmare to the next. We don't speak to each other on our way to the locker room. As I'm changing, Andrew grins at me and whispers, "Nice one with the gum." A few heads lift. Whispers carry. Here's the moment. I could deny it and stay safe and out of trouble. But that would also mean going back to being what's-his-name, the little guy. *Or* I can own it, the good and the bad, and possibly become what I never thought I could be—a legend. Hugo O'Connell, Master Garbologist.

I hold out a fist for Andrew to bump so everybody can see me take the credit. If I'm doing this, I'm going all in. Vij watches me from across the locker room.

When school ends, everyone races through the front doors in a rush to get out in the snow. Vij finds me by my locker.

"Uh, hey, man. I know we got into it back there." He leans against the wall. "But you want to hang after school? I told my mom I had to stay late for the newsletter. If you want, we can sled down the hill behind the soccer field?"

This is how we apologize. It's how it's always been. He knocks me out of the tree he convinced me to climb and then buys me a Popsicle from the ice cream truck to make up for it. I tell his mom he lost the neon yellow scarf she gave him for Christmas and then loan him my favorite Xbox game to pass the time while he's grounded. This is Vij saying sorry for math class and for basically calling me a helpless loser. If I wanted to say sorry for the food fight at lunch, I'd go sledding. But this is different. I'm *not* sorry. Because now I know what he really thinks of me. I'm his poor little cousin who couldn't survive without him. I don't need his pity.

"I can't. Got plans," I say, and yank the zipper of my bag, which is stuck on a torn sheet of paper. Vij reaches out to help, and I jerk away.

He puts his hands up in surrender, and I walk off.

Miracle of miracles, Dad showed up. When I walk down the school steps, he's leaning against the Jeep with two pairs of skis, one extra-long and one extra-short, strapped to the top.

"Are you serious?"

He grins.

"No, really. We're going up the mountain?"

He tosses a duffel bag at me. "Here. Your mother packed it. Dig through and make sure all your gear is there."

I get into the Jeep and hug the bag to me. I'm going skiing on fresh snow before the entire rest of the world. Dad just won back all his Good Dad points.

"Will they even let us on the runs?" I ask, shoving hats and hand warmers aside to hunt for my gloves.

"'They' is 'me,' kid, and I say we go. Check behind your seat. Are those the right size poles?"

I twist around to look behind me at the ski poles zig-zagged across the back seat.

"Buckle," Dad orders, and zooms out of the parking lot.

Mom once got pulled over for speeding, and the police officer also tried to write her up for not having me in a car seat. I was nine. When she explained that I was just really small for my age, the officer had nodded at me and said, "Little guys have it rough." I did not nod back.

"Off we go!" Dad shouts, and hits the roundabout too fast. People lay on their horns, but he rolls down his window and gives them a friendly wave. The wind whips the flags that mark the resort entrance to the mountain.

"Hey, Dad?"

"Yeah?" He's fiddling with the radio, eyes on the dial instead of the road. Mom hates it when he does that.

"What do you actually *do*?"

He finds a Beastie Boys song and cranks it up.

"What do you mean?"

"I mean for your job!" I yell over the noise.

"Well, my official title is 'intermediate ski instructor and lift technician.'"

"So you teach ski lessons and grease the lift?" Wow. And for this we gave up our whole lives? But he's grinning like I just nominated him president of the mountain.

"I get to help people be better skiers and also run analytics on the lifts to make sure they're operating correctly so everyone stays safe. It's the best of both worlds!" He thumps the steering wheel along with the bass. "Though your mother would argue it's not the best use of my engineering degree."

I silently agree. It doesn't seem like something you'd move your family all the way across the state for.

He turns off the radio and looks at me sideways. "Did you know I made it to Eagle Scout in high school?" he asks.

"What, like the king of the Boy Scouts?"

"Pretty much. I earned my twenty-first merit badge my junior year. I can start a fire with almost anything." He laughs.

I never made it to Boy Scout. I had to drop out at Cub level because I couldn't do a lot of the physical challenges, being half the size of the rest of the boys in my troupe. He didn't make it a big deal at the time, but now I wonder if he was secretly disappointed in me. I sink down in my seat.

"I loved the service badges the most, the ones I earned

for good citizenship—first aid and community service," he says now. "The Eagle Scout ceremony was on a Friday afternoon, and your grandparents couldn't come. They both worked for the school district and couldn't get time off. Did you know your grandma drove a bus?"

I flip the seat warmer on, off, on, off, trying to picture Grandma Rose in her Broncos sweatshirt and Keds driving a big yellow bus.

"They were excited for me, but they never really understood why I liked the Scouts so much." He pushes up his glasses. "When I got a full scholarship to college, they expected me to do something practical that would earn a steady paycheck, like Uncle Dave with his business degree. They didn't want us to have to work as hard as they did to provide for our families." Dad shrugs. "So, I majored in computer engineering. But I never stopped skiing. I'd volunteer to teach other students at the university to ski in exchange for a ride out to the mountains. It's how I met your mom, actually."

He cracks the windows, and the cold swirls in, chasing the hot air around the car. I can't picture Mom letting Dad teach her *anything*.

"The mountain is beautiful, Hugo, but it can be intimidating. When I teach people how to ski, I help them be brave. You should have seen the look on your mom's face when she let go of my hand and skied a full run without falling. You don't get those kinds of looks in IT work, believe me."

I do believe him. And I can see how much happier he is. But I'm still on Grandma Rose's side. Do your job and be an Eagle Scout on the weekends. Don't toss your kid to the wolves just so you can "follow your bliss" or whatever.

How can I say that now, though, as Dad flashes his badge at the resort gates and the attendant waves us into Creekside? I'm about to get an all-access pass to the mountain. Free skiing on wide-open runs.

After squeezing into a spot in the Hilton's parking garage, we lug all our gear onto the sidewalk, and I look around. I forget how different it is up here. Down below, you've got all your normal stuff: Kroger, Walgreens, school, traffic, neighborhoods with houses and bits of scraggly yard. Up here it's like a Swiss village. A rich Swiss village. The streets are cobblestone and closed off to cars. The ice-skating rink is open all winter *and* summer. The condos have copper gutters and iron balconies and window boxes of fake wildflowers. Forget Rite Aid; the wooden sign above the drugstore reads APOTHECARY. And for just twenty bucks, you can buy a special "s'mores roasting kit" for the firepit behind the Hilton.

Dad carries the skis and I carry the bag toward the ski rental shop. At least for today, I belong here.

"That's new." I point to a bronze statue of a black bear near the ice-skating rink.

"Yes, they *do* like their upgrades," Dad says and winks.

He scans his employee ID card to get us into the locker room at the rental place, and we change fast. We might have super-secret access to the mountain, but there's still only about an hour of daylight left. We do the awkward robot walk in our ski boots up to the chairlift. When I clip into my skis, it feels like slipping on an old pair of shoes. I may not have made it to Eagle Scout, but at least I can ski.

While Dad's still knocking the snow from his buckles, I push off with my poles and glide forward a foot or two. It's so smooth. I look down at my K2s. They're my favorite skis I've ever owned. Bright neon yellow with black stripes across the back. On the mountain, it doesn't matter how small I am. In these skis, I'm uncatchable.

The lift operator says, "Hey, Sean. Got a hitchhiker?"

Dad nods. "My son, Hugo!"

"Hugo, my man!" he says, and we high-five. He yells at Dad over the sound of the lift motors: "Good powder up top, but it's patchy lower down! Watch yourself on Strawberry Hill!" And then he slows down the lift long enough for us to hop on.

I've never told anyone this, but the chairlift is one of my favorite parts of skiing. Humans should not be allowed to float, suspended by nothing but a wire, hundreds of feet above ground. It's a dare to the laws of physics.

When I was little, I'd pretend I was an explorer in search of animal tracks below. And if Mom went in early for the day, Dad and I would keep a lookout for her purple ski suit as she finished her last run. She'd shout up, "Hello, boys!" and we'd yell down, "Hello, girl!" and wave like crazy.

The setting sun turns the mountain orange as we get off at the top. With nobody else around, it feels like an alien planet. The winds whirl the fresh snow into miniature tornados along the top of the peak. They whirl across our path and hurl themselves into the trees below.

Dad turns toward me, and I see my red woolly hat reflected in the blue mirrors of his glasses. "Easy, medium, or hard?" he asks.

"Medium-hard," I answer.

He grins. "Ready?"

"Ready."

We push off at the same time, and the snow is soft and clean and the mountain silent except for the air whistling by my ears as we speed down the blue run. It's smooth powder all the way down. Dad makes wide turns, slicing the first tracks across the mountain so I can follow. It's *really* hard to question his life choices when this is what I get out of it.

We get five runs in before it's too dark to tell tree from shadow. With the heater cranked on high and our noses dripping, we take our time driving home.

"Do you remember bike-sledding?" Dad asks as we go back around the roundabout and return to the normal world—neon Subway sign, the St. Stephen's steeple lit up by streetlights, the half-full parking lot of a Walmart.

"Of course I do."

The Christmas when I was six, both Aunt Soniah and Uncle Dave got the flu and were too sick to travel. We couldn't go on our annual family ski trip—the one time a year Dad takes a full week off work. Vij and all his sisters were up here, and I was stuck in Denver. It was like Christmas itself was canceled. I was moping on the couch in my pajamas on Christmas Eve when I heard a bell ringing outside and Mom told me to check the front door. Dad was on the sidewalk, straddling his bike with our old red sled tied to the back. "Get your coat!" he said. I looked back to Mom, the family safety monitor. She held out my ski coat and buckled my helmet so it wouldn't pinch.

We rode to the coffee shop on Main Street, where Dad bought me a cider and a brownie even though we hadn't eaten dinner yet. I spun on a stool in my pajamas and ate as slowly as possible to make it last. Then we rode back. I can still feel the bump of the sled over the ice and gravel.

"That was probably not the safest parenting move," he says now, his cheeks as red as his hair from the cold.

"I'm surprised Mom let us do it."

"You should have heard the fight she put up when I dragged out the bungee cord. That's why you had to wear the reflective vest."

"It was worth it."

A few seconds of comfortable silence pass, and then, like a cut to commercial, Dad's whole tone switches as he says, "Listen, Hugo. I know I haven't been around as much as I promised I'd be."

Understatement of the year.

"There's always a lot to learn when you start a new job, and this one more than most. I had to get recertified in CPR, and memorize the lift procedures and the emergency protocols before the mountain officially opens. But that's ending. I'll be home more. We'll find our new normal, okay?"

What was old normal? Dinner around the table would be nice. Maybe it'll happen.

When we pull into our driveway, Mom is standing on the porch in her slippers and jacket. She looks happy. Like, really happy. She waves at us . . . with a hammer. When we walk in, I see why. There's finally something hung in the hallway: her psychology diploma. Our new normal.

Chapter Seven

Two Kinds of People

The floor of my room is arctic this morning. My toes go numb on the sprint to the bathroom. One day Mom and Dad will find me down here, frozen solid underneath my Star Wars blanket, and regret their life choices.

When I get upstairs, the duffel bag from our ski trip yesterday is still by the front door. I can't believe it. He's actually going to walk me to the bus stop two days in a row. It's a new record. I start to smile, then check the coatrack. His puffer's gone. Anger wipes the grin off. He couldn't even make it *one* day.

"Good! You're dressed!" Mom hops down the hallway unsuccessfully trying to pull her shoe on. "Here, take this." She hands me a Pop-Tart and a PediaSure. The bunny slippers are nowhere to be seen. She's in work clothes. I take the Pop-Tart but leave the drink. She doesn't notice.

"You look . . . different."

She glances down at herself.

"It can't be *that* different. I've worn this outfit to work at least a dozen times."

"So you're going back to work today?"

"Well," she says, finally wiggling her foot into her high heel, "technically, the work is coming to me. My first client is due in"—she checks her watch—"twenty minutes!" She throws my backpack at me and opens the door. "Okay! Off you go!"

"This is emotional abandonment, Mom," I call from the front steps. "I feel mentally unsettled by this sudden change." I'm only half kidding.

"I'll see if I can pencil you in for a session at four o'clock." She kisses my head. "Have a lovely day!"

Em is pacing back and forth in front of my locker when I get to school. When she sees me, she motions for me to hurry up instead of waving like a normal person.

"Where have you been? Class starts in seven minutes!"

"Happy Tuesday to you too, Em." To the casual observer she looks exactly like she always does—jeans, sweatshirt, hair pulled back so tight it looks like it hurts. But I am not the casual observer. Her sweatshirt's a little rumpled and there are wisps of hair sticking straight up from her ponytail like exclamation marks. I wonder if something's up at home? Is it her mom? She came to school again last week, during lunch this time, asking Em if she knew which site her dad was working construction on that day because she couldn't get in touch with him and she was late to pick him up. Then she handed her a Carl's Jr. double cheeseburger. Em buried her head in her hands while the rest of the cafeteria looked on. "Mom, I don't even eat meat," she moaned. I thought the heart-shaped sandwich and note were bad. But nobody wants their mother actually *showing up* in the middle of the cafeteria.

"Is everything okay . . . at home?" I pause, unsure what I'm even asking.

"What?" Em narrows her eyes. "Yes, it's fine. What is *not* fine, however, is that the first *Paw Print* goes out on Friday. THIS FRIDAY, Hugo. And Jack hasn't taken a single photo and Gray swears he has but he hasn't uploaded them yet and now Mrs. Jacobsen says the program Micah wants to use to design the layout isn't compatible with the school's computers!" She rubs the side of her head.

"What do you want me to do?"

"*You* need to make sure Vij has his editorial done, and if he hasn't"—she pokes me in the chest—"you're finishing it."

"Em, Vij and I aren't—"

She holds up a hand.

"I don't want to hear it. You two work out your issues

on your own time. I'm done with my exposé on the illegal use of the handicapped parking spaces, of course, but I've got to meet with Mrs. Jacobsen to sort this Micah thing out."

"What Micah thing?" Micah asks, wandering up to us. Today his turtleneck is green.

"Micah, listen—" Em pulls him down the hallway while I use up all my remaining six minute and forty-seven seconds talking to Andrew about his new strategy for winning over Coach, which involves six packs of SlimFast and IcyHot gel for his knee. We pass Jasmine and one of her friends, and they *both* smile at me, and I forget everything Andrew is saying to me and everything Em told me to do.

Then I walk into English and see Vij—already in his seat, head down, hood up—and I remember Em told me I have to play nice. I sit.

Without turning around, I say, "Em's on the warpath. You've got to turn in your editorial."

"Got it."

"Good. Because *I'm* not writing it."

And that is the end of our social interaction. But it's only the start to my backward day where my cousin won't talk to me but everybody *else* does. Word of the Garbologist—solver of mysteries, matchmaker, game changer—has gotten around. Two seventh-grade boys slip me a Ziploc stuffed with Mr. Lutz's trash. They're trying to pass life science. A girl in my Spanish class hands me a paper bag filled with things she collected from the floor of her brother's car. She wants me to tell her how to get him to give her rides more often so she won't have to take the bus. When we get to lunch, Jasmine and the rest of the girls' soccer team wave at me long enough to make me trip over my own foot and bump into Em, who spills her barbecue chickpea puffs all over the table.

She huffs and I help her pick them all up, conveniently letting Micah take my spot when Vij arrives.

Em lunges over me toward him. "Did you finish?"

"I'll have it done by the end of today," he says without looking at her.

"End of today like end of *school*. Not end of today like midnight, right?"

"*Chill*, Em. You'll *get* it," Vij says. "Why can't you ever relax?"

Em shrinks back.

"Dude, easy," I say, and Vij finally turns to me.

"Heard you did a little night skiing."

He's mad I went without him. Like I owe him *anything*.

"Who told you?"

"My dad." Vij stirs his fruit salad until it dissolves into a puddle of pink-and-green mush. Gray takes a picture of it.

"That is not on the list of required shots," Em barks. He

snaps one of her, and she shields her eyes like a vampire.

"You got first run at the mountain?" Jack asks. "I bet it was insane."

Vij snorts.

"You know what? Yeah, it was awesome. Best snow I've ever skied. Powder at the top. No slush or ice at the bottom. And no lift lines." I sit back in my seat. "If you're gonna ski, that's the way to do it."

Vij opens his mouth to say something, but Em slaps her hand down on the table.

"Enough! We need to strategize!" She talks at us for the rest of lunch, which is fine by me because then I don't have to look at Vij.

Maybe it's because of all the weirdness at lunch, but I forget to prepare myself for gym. I forget about Chance. Everyone knows that the minute you forget about the monster, the monster appears.

My shoelaces have somehow twisted themselves into such a complicated knot that I have to sit down to untangle them. Except the benches are full of everyone else sitting down to put on *their* shoes. I prop my foot up on my locker and try to tug at what I hope is the looser end of the shoelace. It doesn't go well. I lose my balance and take a step back. My heel lands on Chance's toe. Hard.

"Get off!"

He shoves me forward and my shoulder hits the locker. I stay leaning against it—for moral support.

"Sorry! I'm off!"

The room goes silent.

"Are you still learning to walk, baby Hugo?" He leans in close. Under the locker room funk of mold and feet, I can smell him—morning breath that lasts all day and armpit sweat. There's one giant pimple ready to erupt on his forehead. I try to back up, but there's nowhere to go. Across the room, Vij stands still, a spectator like everybody else.

"I said I'm sorry."

"What's that, little man?"

He tilts his ear toward me, and I clear my throat, but the shame sticks.

"I'm *sorry*," I say as loud as I can manage.

He straightens up and I am eye level with his sternum.

"That's okay." He pats me roughly on the shoulder. "I mean, if a baby's just learning to walk, you can't really get *mad* at them when they fall, right, Hugo?"

I don't say anything. I couldn't now if I tried. I keep my eyes on my shoes. I blink and the laces blur. Maybe if I'm still enough, he'll stop.

"Let's give it up for little Hugo, guys! He just took his first step!" Chance starts to slow clap. Clap. Clap. Clap. They hit me like slaps. Clap. *Slap*. Clap. *Slap*. A few basketball guys join in, looking confused. Andrew is at the end of our bench. He doesn't clap, but he doesn't stop it. It's like our walk to class this morning where he couldn't stop thanking me for all my help with Coach never happened. He looks away, just like Vij. It hurts even though I tell myself it shouldn't. How many times have I done the same to Micah? It's harder than it looks to stand up to a bully. Then the worst thing happens—I start to cry. I'm not making noises. It's not that kind of cry, but everyone sees the one tear that escapes before I can scrub it away with the back of my hand. I haven't cried in front of a bully since T-ball.

Chance pauses. Crying is the most humiliating way to stop the teasing—like waving your underwear in surrender. At least it's over. I need to get out of here. The space is too hot and too close. Too many bodies with too much nervous energy. But Chance isn't done. He leans in close and sniffs loudly. "Something *stinks*. You better stop playing in the *trash*, man." Then he rubs my head. "For luck."

I'm the last one to leave the locker room. It's peaceful in here without lockers slamming and toilets flushing. I collapse on the empty bench and work on my shoelace. The knot comes away easily.

Chance basically called me a baby and then *rubbed my head* like a lucky penny in front of everyone. And I let him. It's the diaper helmet in T-ball and being called "Shorts" for *years*. It's every class photo where I have to stand in the front row all the way to the left because they line us up according to size. It's so unfair. I always just stand there and *take* it.

Vij sticks his head around the corner. "Uh, Coach called roll. He wants you out on the court." His voice is quiet. Polite.

"Yeah, got it."

He ducks out and then sticks his head back in. "We're playing dodgeball. You're on my team."

Dodgeball. Of course.

In the gym, Coach is finishing lining up red and yellow rubber balls along the half-court line. The yellow ones are smaller but harder, so they hurt worse. Chance is on the far side, shooting free throws with a red one. Every shot goes in.

I take my place along the baseline. Everyone is careful not to look at me. I've never wanted to hurl a ball at someone more in my life. The sides are pretty evenly matched. Andrew and a couple other tall guys are on this side. It's ten against ten. Coach puts his whistle in his mouth and steps back.

Here's the thing you have to know about dodgeball. It separates the world into two types of people: the ones who know fear and the ones who don't. If you're not scared, those balls lined up neat and tidy along the half-court line are all for you. You hold five at once and throw like a quarterback from baseline to baseline. You don't worry about getting hit, because you know the smaller guys, your wingmen, have got your back. They're dispensable. One goes down, and another fills his place. Their whole job is to protect you, their MVP. You are a machine, and you can take your time picking your target, pacing back and forth underneath the basket like a lion.

But those of us who know fear play the game differently. We know that first dash to half-court isn't for us. We hang back. Maybe a ball will rocket off a foot and roll our way. Maybe it will bounce off the back wall and we'll catch it. But that's not our priority. We're not in it to take people out. We're in it to stay alive. It's all about defense. So we dart and dive and fall to our knees so hard it burns the skin off. Anything to avoid that smack across the shoulder, stomach, shin that means we're done. It's survival.

Mom made me take a personality test once, but I didn't listen to the results. You know all you need to know about yourself after one game of dodgeball.

Coach blows the whistle.

And that's when I decide to be the other guy.

Instead of slinking back, I run straight for the line. I'm faster than I look. I scrabble for three yellows. That's all I can hold. Andrew gets there at the same time and grabs four. Chance is already ahead of us. He's also got four and kicks three more back toward his side, which is illegal, but Coach doesn't call it.

Andrew and I run backward to get some distance. I throw one and miss and then throw another. It just barely nicks the arm of a kid from history class. It's enough. A hit is a hit. He heads to the bench. I get a second out on the butt of someone bending over to pick up a red ball. Easy target. I laugh out loud. Who knew all you needed to do to win was get angry?

"Dude, what?" is all Vij has time to say before he ducks a vicious spiral from Chance that I'm pretty sure was aimed at me. For once, my size is my advantage. Smaller body, smaller target.

"Here." I pass him my last ball and run for more.

I'm bouncing on my toes halfway to the middle of the court before the other side catches on that I'm not playing my usual role. Peter, from English, can't get out of my way fast enough. He goes down with a hit to the knee. From the corner of my eye, I see Chance signal to his wingman. They both march toward me, and I dance back a few feet. Andrew passes me a ball on my left, but before he can get another one for himself, he gets hit and Coach waves him to the sidelines.

"Sorry, man," he calls. The kid that tagged him stands there watching him jog off the court, so I nail him with an easy lob. He looks around, surprised. *You take my guy, I'll take you.*

By now it's down to me and Vij against Chance and Gray. I feel bad for Gray. I'm pretty sure he only plays soccer because of Jack. He once told me he thinks team sports shouldn't keep score. "I just don't see the point," he said, and shook his head, and now Chance is up in his face, yelling "GET THE BALL!" I can see the spit flying. My heart's hammering, but my hands are steady. We each have one ball. This is it.

Chance winds up like a pitcher.

But I release mine first.

His is faster. It whistles through the air.

There's no time to move.

A body flies past me. It's Vij. He dives in front of me like he's sliding into home base. The ball smacks his hand and it echoes like a whip. I look over him, following the arc of my own throw. Chance ducks and it gets Gray square in the stomach.

Vij and Gray take their places on the benches along with the rest of the class. It's down to me and Chance. The sidelines are full and silent. One yellow ball rolls slowly toward me. Chance has one at his feet. He's sweating and grunting and tired. It's the best I can hope for.

For one second we stand there, looking at each other.

Then I dive for my ball and he dives for his.

I scoop it up and release with as much topspin as I can. It's a beautiful throw. A perfect one.

But it's not enough.

I hear the slap of the ball before I feel the sting. Surprise comes first, then the pain. He got me right in the face. My eyes water and the gym floor blurs. Oh, I'm on the floor now. Some kind of liquid is coming out of my face. Blood? Sweat? Snot? All three? Black spots dance in front of my eyes, and I close them and curl up, because a nap seems like the best choice right now. Somewhere far away, Coach is blowing the whistle and yelling, "Foul!" over and over.

Vij walks me to the nurse's office. Like my mom, Nurse Ruby is from Texas. Except unlike my mom, you can really tell. She's got a big accent and even bigger hair.

"Here, hon." She hands me a bag filled with ice and wrapped in a towel. "I know it's cold, but you've got to keep that on there or the swelling's going to turn you black and blue."

"Thanks, Nurse Ruby."

"Sure thing."

She turns to Vij. "You look pretty ragged yourself. Want some juice?"

He shakes his head but grins up at her. Nurse Ruby is new this year and pretty. When she walks out, Vij whispers, "Think you could look in her trash?"

I smile, but it hurts—because of my face, but also because Vij felt like he had to save me on the court. He threw himself in front of the ball to protect little baby Hugo, again. So much for the legend that was the Garbologist.

"Sorry about your shirt," I mumble. A few drops of blood leak out onto the towel.

I'm lying on the cot, and Vij sits in the blue plastic chair near my feet. We look down at the balled-up undershirt in my hands. It's covered in rusty red spots from my bloody nose. Apparently, he donated it to the cause when I was passed out on the gym floor.

"I think the blood is an improvement," he jokes, but then looks out the window. "In the locker room . . . I should have said something. Chance is an idiot."

When it comes to what hurts worse, it's a tie between my nose and the embarrassment.

I close my eyes. "It's cool."

He nudges my foot with his knee, so I look at him.

"Hey, but you're a celebrity now with the whole garbology thing. You have to admit it's pretty awesome."

He's trying to make me feel better, which makes it a thousand times worse. Between what happened in the locker room and my total defeat on the dodgeball court, I lost any credit I'd just built up by being the Garbologist.

"Yeah, the infamous trashman," I say with fake cheer. A dribble of ice water runs down the side of my face and into my ear.

Vij grins and adds, "Star Trash: The Next Generation."

"Oscar the Grouch 2.0."

"King of Compost. No, Master of the Dump!"

Vij salutes me and then shakes his head. "Chance, man. What a waste of *so much* space."

"No kidding," I say, and make myself smile.

Needless to say, Vij did not have his editorial done by the end of school. So Em's making him stay until he finishes. She actually called his mom, which did not go over well with Vij.

Em studies my face like a surgeon. The inside corners of my eyes are already turning purple.

"It happened in gym?" she asks. And then, before I can answer, she says, "It was Chance, wasn't it? Was it on purpose? Did you tell a teacher?"

"I'm fine, Em. It was an accident in dodgeball."

She narrows her eyes but lets me go. I walk out to the bus stop and let the freezing air numb my face.

All I want to do when I get home is lie on my bed and watch reruns of *The Simpsons*, but Mom meets me on the porch and clamps her hands on my shoulders like a security guard. "Tell me what happened."

I bet she already knows. The school totally called her, and this is one of her therapy tricks to see if my story matches up with theirs.

"Nothing, Mom. I'm fine. It was an accident in gym. Do we have any Thin Mints left?" I try to sidestep her, but she moves right as I move left and blocks me. Her hands are still on my shoulders, like a super awkward mother-son slow dance.

"Thin Mints, yes. Go down to your room and rest, and I'll bring some to you."

Between Vij and Em and now Mom, pretty much the whole world has decided I can't look after myself. But wait, something's off. After the week-old tuna sandwich incident, Mom made a new rule: no food outside the kitchen. She never breaks her own rules. So why is she letting me eat the world's most crumbly cookie in bed? She glances over her shoulder into the house.

"Why are you being weird?"

"I'm not."

"You *are*."

She sighs and shuts the door behind her.

"The thing is, Hugo, one of my earlier sessions had to reschedule for this afternoon."

"This afternoon, like . . . *now*?" I stand on my tiptoes to look inside the living room window, but everything's in shadow.

"I'm so sorry. I'll just be another half hour. Are you okay to hang in your room?"

That's the only place I wanted to go until she said I had to. Now it feels like punishment. I nod anyway.

"Thanks, love." She speed walks me down the hall and to the basement. Then she kisses me on my bruised nose before gently slamming the door in my face.

Chapter Eight

Read All About It!

Is it bad form to shove yourself into your own locker? Because on this totally regrettable morning after dodgeball, I would if I could. Behind me, I hear sounds of life—the buzz of the intercom as Ms. Lancy warms up for morning announcements and people laughing at videos on their phones until the very last second they have to put them away. All I have to do is turn around, keep my head down, and march myself to English class, but I can't do it. I can't show my face after the double whammy of humiliation that was gym class yesterday.

I take a deep breath, which hurts my nose, and then another one for good measure and slam my locker shut. I pretend I am playing a game of Pokémon GO, except I am the Pokémon and my one objective is to not get caught. I am on the very threshold of English class when Peter, fellow dodgeballer and classmate, stops me.

"Hey, Hugo, you left this."

He holds out my English notebook with the cover half peeling off and notes Vij and I have passed back and forth slipping out. I must have dropped it in my panicky flight from my locker.

"Thanks," I mumble, keeping my swollen nose pointed at the floor.

His red Chuck Taylors don't move.

"Nice moves at the game, by the way," he says.

I look up to check if he's joking. "What?" I got nailed in the face and bled all over the court. He has to be messing with me.

"You played a good game. I know I was on Chance's team, but we were all rooting for you," he adds, and hitches his bag higher on his shoulders. Peter is one of those kids you forget to remember. He's always somewhere in the crowd blending in, never quite in the front and never all the way in the back, either. Suddenly his opinion means everything.

"Really?"

"Yeah, we were all talking about it."

"But I didn't win."

"Yeah, but we've never seen Chance sweat so hard." He grins. "It was sweet."

"Gentlemen," Mrs. Jacobsen calls from her desk. "Inside, please."

I pretend not to hear.

"Well, I thought he could use a little exercise," I say, and we both laugh.

"Boys, *now*," Mrs. Jacobsen orders, and we start walking. But before I can get to my seat, Peter whispers, "Hey, I've got this guy on my hockey team who won't stop harassing me for my slap shots. You think I could bring you his game-day trash and you could help me out?"

I don't even slow my walk, just bump his fist with mine, slide into my seat while Vij watches, and say, at full volume, "I got you, man."

The Garbologist is back.

By Friday my nose is back to normal size but not color. The purple has faded to a nice boggy green. I look haunted. But nothing compares to Em's face right before first period. She's exactly the shade of the October sky, which is so pale and white it's almost gray. The word "ashen" in our vocab books finally makes sense.

"Micah double-checked that the picture of the parking lot is horizontal, not vertical, right?" she asks before I can even get through my locker combination.

"I'm sure he did."

"But yesterday after school it kept defaulting to vertical and cutting into the column." She's tugging at her jacket sleeves, pulling them down over her hands. The minute she lets go they slide up and then she does it again.

"Em, I'm sure Mrs. Jacobsen checked that it was right."

"But that's not her job, Hugo! She's the supervisor, not part of the staff. It's *my* job as editor-in-chief to make sure every single piece is perfect by print day and I CAN'T REMEMBER IF THE PARKING LOT SHOT WAS HORIZONTAL OR VERTICAL!"

"Stop yelling. It was horizontal." I yank my locker open and grab the first three things that fall out, hoping one of them is my English book.

"You're positive?"

"Positive." I shove her toward her class. I actually have no idea whether the picture was right or not, but the newsletter's already printed. There's nothing God or Em can do about it now. I slap Peter and Andrew on their backs on my way to English, and we walk in together. Vij comes in half a minute later as the bell is ringing. I forgot I told him I'd wait for him by the lockers. He takes his seat as Mrs. Jacobsen begins passing out the reading quiz. I whisper, "Sorry, man" and don't get a response. When I start to turn around, Mrs. Jacobsen orders, "Eyes on your own paper," so I'm stuck. I'm sure he's fine. It's not like we *always* walk to class together.

I fall asleep in Spanish. It's because Dad woke me up last night when he dropped his ski boots in the upstairs hallway. He and Mom stayed up most of the night doing that angry-whisper thing they do, which is actually louder than if they talked normally.

He still can't manage to get home for dinner. The ski day feels like years ago—a different life, a different Dad. How many promises do you break until no one believes you anymore? Whatever number that is, he's one past it. I thought Mom would be happier now that she's working, but it's just given her ammunition to point out all the ways Dad *isn't* stepping up. The way they look at each other lately makes my stomach ache. I keep myself distracted with garbology assignments. People have started messaging me with their requests. I've never had so many contacts in my phone before. My room, however, is starting to look like the dumpster behind McDonald's.

I'm so busy trying to stay awake through my classes, I forget all about the *Paw Print* until lunch. Em and Micah are standing by the lunch line passing out the newsletter we printed on bright yellow paper. Gray and Jack man the double doors that open out into the main hallway. They're kind of *tossing* them at people. Vij and I were supposed to be here early to help, but I got held up by the girl whose brother still won't give her a ride to school. I told her there's only so much a garbologist can do. She'll have to do the rest herself. I rush over to Em, who glares and thrusts a pile at me. Without a word, she points at Vij, who's standing at our appointed spot near the trash cans.

She is equal parts furious at me for being late and nervous because she's been working toward this moment since the first day of school. I shoot her a thumbs-up, which she ignores, and walk dutifully over to Vij, who gives me a nod without really looking at me. He can't be mad that I'm late, can he? He's *always* late.

We're not getting a lot of traffic. Everyone's busy eating their tomato soup and grilled cheese. I wish I could have at least grabbed a sandwich. For once the cafeteria smells delicious. When her line empties, Em comes over with Micah and hovers behind us.

"Em," Vij says without turning around, "you're being creepy."

"Hush, here come some people," she whispers.

A seventh grader in a striped sweater dumps her trash in the bin and smiles at me. I recognize her from one of the bags of trash in my bedroom. She's trying to convince her mom to get her a dog. It's not looking good from all the tissues and the empty Claritin bottle in the bottom of the bag. I smile back at her until Em clears her throat and nudges me. I try to hand the girl a flyer, but she says, "No, thanks" and leaves. The same thing happens over and over again as people clear the room. Vij only gets one taker, and it's one of the cafeteria workers who says, "Thank you, dear" before returning to the soup station. Micah picks up a few from the ground and begins to straighten them. So far the reception has been . . . less than enthusiastic. I didn't really contribute anything to the newsletter, other than following Vij around and helping Gray shrink his JPEGs. I've been elbows-deep in trash and haven't had time to help as much as I promised. Now it's tanking, and I wish I could get a do-over, anything to help Em. Behind me she is silent. I'm psyching myself up to turn around and look at her when Chance wanders over.

"What happened to your face, O'Connell? Did you walk into a wall or something?" Clever.

He leans over to Vij.

"What you got there?" He pronounces it "watchoo."

Vij doesn't respond, so Chance grabs the entire stack out of his hands.

"Hey!" Em yelps. He doesn't acknowledge her. As he studies the newsletter, my stomach curls into a ball and retreats somewhere behind my spleen.

He starts reading aloud: "According to state statutes determined by the Americans with Disabilities Act," he says, "public buildings are required to provide one handicapped parking space per twenty-five regular spaces." Surely, he's done. No, he keeps going. "When a vehicle illegally takes up one of the few available spaces—" Now he stops and looks up at us, genuinely confused.

"Are you kidding me? You wrote an entire newsletter about *parking spaces*?"

Em steps forward. "Actually, we also wrote about the new water bottle stations, and there's a calendar of upcoming events, and if you look on the back"—she reaches out and flips one of the sheets over—"you'll see a feature article on Mr. Carpenter, who's retiring at the end of this year."

Chance's big head swivels toward Em. "It says that, does it? About Mr. Carpenter?"

Em nods. My pulse lurches. She hasn't had years of experience with this like I have. She hasn't learned to anticipate it. She won't know to brace herself for whatever comes next. It'll be the worst kind of free fall. I open my mouth to warn her, but nothing comes out.

Chance tips the entire stack into the trash. "Oops."

Em sucks in a sharp breath, and I feel it like a punch, because yeah, Chance did a terrible thing, but I'm the one being a coward about it. Now. Now is when I should tell Chance that was totally uncool. Except the longer he stands here staring down at us, the smaller I feel.

"Chance! Vijay! Hugo! Emilia! Micah! All of you *get to class*!" Mr. Wahl bellows from the other end of the cafeteria.

Chance begins to whistle and strolls away. Em takes two tiny steps forward and peers down into the trash can. Splashes of soup and blobs of cheese spackle her newsletters. It looks like a crime scene. She stares down at them for a long time.

"Em—"

She holds up her hand like a teacher calling for silence. Eventually she lifts her head and turns toward the empty cafeteria. Vij and I follow her gaze. Yellow sheets lay crumpled on the floor and on the tables. A few poke out of the recycle bin. Somehow there seem to be more on the ground than came from the printer. I clear my throat, hoping the right words will follow, but nothing comes.

The bell rings.

"Ms. Costa. Mr. Rosen. The Misters O'Connell," Mr. Wahl says, close to my ear. I jump. "You are now late for class." He pulls out his green pad. "You will all report to detention this afternoon."

This has to be the first time in her life that Em's gotten in trouble, but she takes her slip without looking at it. That makes me more worried about her than anything else.

"Come on, Em, let's go," Vij says, tugging at her sleeve until she starts moving.

Mrs. Jacobsen is on detention duty. She lets Vij and Micah and me listen to music on my phone once we show her we're done with our homework. Em, though, sits for twenty minutes without moving. I check to see if she's blinking, but my own eyes start to water before I can make sure. Mrs. Jacobsen calls her to her desk. She takes off her glasses and folds them in her hands.

Then she starts talking very quickly and quietly. I can't hear what she's saying, and Em doesn't respond. She sits, tearing a blank piece of paper into shreds and then rolling those shreds into teeny tiny balls. Twice, Mrs. Jacobsen pauses and waits for a response, but Em says nothing. Her face stays blank. It's like she's hiding behind a forcefield of her own Em-ness. Mrs. Jacobsen isn't getting through. But I'm going to try. I didn't do my job as her friend and stand up to Chance with her, back there in the cafeteria. I've had all detention to think of an idea—something that can't totally make it up to her, but at least might help.

I text Dad under the table to ask for a favor. I don't want to ask him for anything after his marathon fight with Mom last night, but the way I figure it, he owes me one, or a million. I'm shocked when he responds almost immediately—two thumbs-up and a smiley face. His guilt is working in my favor. I text Mom next and tell her I'll be home by six, but I don't say why because she would 100 percent say no. You gotta know which parent to work.

Vij leans over my shoulder and reads my text to Mom. "Where're you off to?"

"*We*, my friends," I say to Vij and Micah, "are going on a little trip."

Micah yells, "Awesome!" and gets shushed by Mrs. Jacobsen, but Vij raises his eyebrows like he doesn't believe me. What? I flake out on him a couple of times and now I've lost all credibility?

"Seriously. Get your stuff after this and meet me by the front doors."

Once we're dismissed, I walk over to where Em's zipping up her bag.

"Hey." I tap her on the shoulder. She doesn't look at me.

"Um, when do you have to be home?"

"Well," she says slowly, standing up and hitching her bag higher on her back. "This morning I told my mom I was staying late to start planning next month's newsletter, but she's probably already forgotten, and there doesn't seem to be any point, so . . ." she trails off. It's worse than I thought. She's lost the will to work.

"So no plans, then? Good. You're coming with me." I grab hold of her backpack strap and yank. She has no choice but to follow. We walk like this, with me holding the strap, all the way to the front steps, where Vij and Micah are waiting. As we cut across the parking lot toward the main street, Em finally catches on that we're about to leave school property. She jerks to a stop.

"Where are we going?"

"Don't you trust me?" I ask.

"Not even a little."

"I *swear* you will be home by six." I hold up three fingers and then two because I can't remember what the Boy

Scouts' hand signal is—this is why I never made it past Cubs.

"Fine," she sighs, but her eyes go wide when the public bus pulls up and we begin to file on.

She pauses at the bottom step.

"Just . . . *trust* me, okay?"

She looks back toward the school and then at me and then back to the school. Then she pulls her ponytail as tight as it will go and steps up onto the bus.

If I thought it was a different world at Creekside when Dad and I came up before, it's like the North Pole meets Hogwarts meets the Macy's Thanksgiving Day Parade now. Opening weekend at a ski resort is a thing to behold. The bronze black bear has a wreath around its neck. Giant bows hang from every lamppost, and lights twinkle in the flower boxes on the balconies. Musicians play on a platform in front of the ice-skating rink. They have big long horns and fiddles, and it feels like we're on the set of *The Sound of Music*.

The place is packed. Women in high-heeled boots and fur coats tiptoe over patches of ice. Men sit around the firepits smoking cigars and barking with laughter. The workers—the baristas and rink assistants and shopkeepers, the ones who keep this place running—blend into the background. There's never been such a clear line between those who have and those who most definitely have not. Tourist season has begun.

Em lets me lead her through the crowd and up two escalators to the ski rental shop. Dad is waiting inside. His cheeks are red, and his hair is a total disaster. He must have just come off the mountain.

She pulls me aside. "We get free skiing on the mountain? *Opening day* free skiing?"

I nod.

She doesn't say anything. *Good surprise or bad surprise?* I want to ask, while she stares at me. I can read almost anybody's trash, but I cannot read Em's face.

"All right, I've got skis and boots for Hugo and Vij, but Emilia and Micah, you're going to have to tell me your sizes. We'll see what we've got in the back." He puts his hand on the counter like he's about to take their order at Subway. Vij grabs his boots, grinning like it's Christmas come early. I guess all is forgiven from earlier. I am beyond grateful Dad already has my boots out so Em doesn't have to hear me say my shoe size. I've never liked telling people what size clothes or shoes I wear. It shouldn't matter, but it does.

She says, "Umm, I'm usually a five, sir, but I'm not sure I should be—"

"Nonsense." Dad claps his hands together. "I called your mother. Yours too, Vij, and your grandmother, Micah.

We're all on the up-and-up. Now let me see if I can find those fives." He doesn't mention calling Mom.

Once we're geared up, Dad escorts us to the chairlift and tells the operator to "take care of them," before waving us off. No self-respecting Coloradoan would ski in jeans, but it's all we've got, and once we're on the lift, I don't even feel the cold. I look over to Em on my right. She's smiling. Like a real smile. So, *good* surprise, then. Micah, on her other side, adjusts his glasses and leans over the rail. I bet if his dad were here, he'd take him on the mountain all the time.

Vij starts to rock our chair back and forth. It swings and creaks in the wind.

"Cut it out." I shove him hard enough that he almost drops his gloves.

"You cut it out." He pushes me back and I knock into Em who knocks into Micah.

"*Both* of you cut it out," she says, but she's laughing. I think this might be the first time she's looked more like an eleven-year-old than a mini-mom.

The lift stops halfway up. Somebody probably lost a ski or is too scared to get on or too slow to get off. Vij stops rocking. My boots are a little too big with my thin socks. My heels rub up and down each time I shift my skis. Now that we're still, I start to shiver. I hope we get moving soon.

"It's not just Chance, you know," Em says into the silence.

"What's not Chance?" Micah asks.

"Nobody read the newsletter."

Vij and I trade glances.

"People took them," she says mostly to herself, "but then they dropped them on the floor, or left them at their table. I saw one girl spit her gum in it."

"Maybe it's because it's Friday and everybody's thinking about the weekend and ski season opening and—"

"No," Em says, cutting me off, "it's not that. Nobody wants to read about parking spaces and drinking fountains and what Mr. Carpenter majored in in college."

"I do!" Micah offers up.

"No." She shakes her head. "Even my mom forgot it was today. I wrote it on the calendar on the fridge, and I thought maybe she'd do something special, you know? Like make breakfast or call me after school to ask about it, but . . ." She pauses. "It's not her fault. She works two jobs, and my parents share a car. It doesn't matter. Chance was right. Nobody cares."

"Whoa." Vij holds up a hand. "Let's not get crazy. Chance is *never* right." Then he adds gently, "We just need to spice it up."

Em twists her hands around the safety bar.

"Next time will be amazing," he adds. "We'll sell out!

This was a warm-up. That's it. Not everyone can get it right *every* time. Not even you, Em."

"We can do it," Micah says, sounding even more sure than Vij.

"They're right," I add. "We've got a month. I'll help more this time. I'll write whatever you want. I swear. It'll be great."

Em settles back against the cold vinyl seat.

"You really think so?" she asks finally.

"I do."

The chairlift starts moving again with a jerk. Up above, we can see the top of the mountain coming into view. This is it. We're about to ski the mountain, without responsible adults, on opening day. Vij claps his gloved hands together and howls like a wolf. After a second, I do too and so does Micah. It's something we'd get made fun of for if Chance or anyone else heard, but out here there's nothing but us and the open air. I howl so loud my ears pop. Em even joins in with a little "yip yip, yeooowwww!" We howl all the way to the top.

"Micah, I cannot believe how fast you took those moguls!" Vij yells when we slide to a stop after our first run. He's right. Micah was like a cheetah on skis, his legs moving at warp speed over the icy mounds.

He plants his poles in the ground to receive all our high fives. Then he shrugs.

"We basically live on the slopes when my dad is here."

As we get in line for the chairlift, I ask, though I'm not sure if I should, "When—when is your dad supposed to get back?"

"His deployment was scheduled to last six months, but it got extended to nine, so, February, but my granny says Easter if we're lucky." He rubs at his glasses to clear some of the fog, and whatever he sees in my face before I can cover it up makes him hurry to add, "But the zone he's in is mostly stable! He said in his last email they'd even started a baseball league."

I plaster on a grin, and he smiles back. Except all I'm thinking is that I complain about Dad not making it home for *dinner*. I can't imagine months without him and not knowing when he'll get back. *If* he'll get back. Micah inches forward with his poles as the line moves. He's the toughest of all of us.

Three runs are all we can squeeze in before it's last call for the chairlift and time to catch the shuttle back down to town. While we wait, Em leans over and whispers, "Thank you, Hugo" and hugs me, and my brain short circuits and I forget what my arms are supposed to do. On the ride down, our noses are running and nobody has tissues and Micah's glasses are completely fogged over again and my jeans are soaked through and my heel definitely has a blister.

But it was totally worth it.

At least it *was* until Aunt Soniah drops me off at home.

The shuttle took longer than usual to get us down because of all the extra people and all the extra stops on opening day. It is 6:47 when I walk through the front door and dump my wet jacket on the floor.

"So is it shrimp, tuna, or salmon?" I yell down the hall, because that's the only way we know how to do fish Friday. But the fishy smell is mysteriously absent. The house is quiet. Creepy quiet. All the lights are off except for in the kitchen. I follow its glow down the hallway, peeling off my damp socks along the way. Mom sits at the table in her fuzzy robe with her back to me. She doesn't turn even when I walk up right next to her. Her hands are clasped in front of her and her eyes are closed. For a second I think she's praying, but then she huffs out a breath, opens her eyes, and points to the clock.

"I can explain."

"Don't."

"Em was having a bad day."

"So you decide to take the shuttle *by yourself.* And ride the chairlift *by yourself.* And ski down the mountain *by yourself!*"

"Dad said it was okay."

"*Dad* said it was okay?!" She stands up and marches past me. I follow her down the hall at a safe distance. She picks up my wet socks and hurls them into the laundry basket and then jams my jacket onto the hook by the door. Then she turns toward me.

"Let me ask you something, Hugo. Why didn't you check with *me*?"

"I, uh, needed Dad to get us boots and skis and stuff."

She crosses her arms. "Try again."

"I knew you were busy with clients."

She shakes her head.

"Okay. I just didn't think about it!"

"No." She points a finger in my face. "You knew I'd say no, so you went to your father who is so *distracted* with his new job that he didn't stop to think about your safety! I had to hear about it from your aunt!" She stops. Breathes in for four. Yanks her robe tighter. And breathes out.

"Go change your clothes," she says in a new voice. "There's leftover lasagna in the fridge."

"What about fish Friday?" I ask as she turns to walk back down the hallway. Mom never leaves first. She's always grabbing my sleeve or calling me back for one more thing. I lean against the wall in the dark and feel more alone than if the house were empty. As she disappears around the corner, I shout, "I was just trying to be nice!" But she's already gone.

Chapter Nine

....

Breaking and Entering

Mom seemed back to normal on Sunday morning. She even made pancakes with chocolate chips for the two of us. Dad, of course, was on the mountain. But then she didn't let me go over to Vij's after Mass, and every time I walked out of a room, she asked me where I was going. So, not totally back to normal. It was like she grounded me without ever actually saying it.

Her fight with Dad on Friday night began with an epic round of hissing whispers after they thought I'd gone to bed, and it ended with him on the couch, where he has spent the last three nights. They've fought a million times since we've moved here, but they've never slept apart. I kicked his pillow off the end of the couch this morning and then carried it back into their room and put it on his side of the bed. That pillow being in the living room terrifies me more than the entire move from Denver.

I can't stop seeing Em's face as she stared at the flyers in the trash can and tried not to cry. I can't unhear Mom yelling at Dad. And my nose *still* hurts. It's Monday now, and I've had the weekend to think about it. If you trace the line of events all the way back, there's only one conclusion: This is completely Chance's fault. He is ruining my life and the lives of my friends. It's time to fight back.

I pull Vij aside before he can walk into English.

"I have a plan."

"Yeah? For the next *Paw Print*?" he asks.

"What? No. I have a *plan*"—I lean in close to his ear—"related to garbology and *revenge*."

Em is in better spirits this week. She greets us at lunch with a list, front and back, of new ideas for the next issue, and she wants us to put our initials by the assignments we want. She's jotted down things like:

New turf on soccer field
Recent study on concussion in youth hockey
ebook vs hard copy (English class debate????)
Cougar mascot—too violent, vote to rename?
Childcare for teachers
Organic snacks in vending machine (poll??)

We all kind of say "hmmm" and "yeah, maybe" but nobody initials anything, not even Micah. Meanwhile, Vij and I are in a text debate and hiding our phones under the table.

Vij: today after school

Me: cant. mom making me go straight home

Vij: tmrw before lunch after algebra

Me: no he's IN that class and the crow will never let us both leave early

Vij: 😒

Vij: U figure it out then

Me: (after a few seconds where Em definitely gives me a dirty look during her cost analysis of Annie's Organic Cheddar Squares versus regular Cheez-Its) fri right after school during bball practice

Vij:

"Dude," I say out loud, "please never use the winking face again." Em takes our phones away for the rest of lunch.

The week passes as slowly as humanly possible. Seriously. It's like counting down to Christmas. There's a bright spot on Wednesday when the girl in my Spanish class brings me homemade blueberry muffins for looking through her brother's car trash. He's *finally* driving her to school now.

After the bell rings at the end of the day on Friday, I meet Vij at our pre-planned location behind the school. I'm late after being stopped again for more garbology-related business. I had to reject four bags for hygienic reasons, and the owners were not happy. It took a while to sort out. I was afraid Vij would have given up and left, but he's there, kicking dirty icicles off the bottom of the dumpsters.

"Did you make sure everyone saw you leave through the front doors?" I ask him.

"Of *course* I did."

"Easy. I'm just checking. What time is it?"

He checks his phone. "It's 4:05."

"Okay, we'll give it another few minutes. Make sure practice has already started and everyone's in the gym."

I kick one of the icicles he's already broken off and we kind of pass it back and forth for a while until it breaks into a thousand pieces. I'm starting to think this is a bad idea. I mean, this week's been pretty good. Chance only rubbed my head for luck twice. Em's happily ordering everyone around again. The Crow hasn't singled me or Vij or Micah out once. Mom even let Dad back into their bedroom yesterday.

I almost tell Vij we should call it off, go get fries at Five Guys instead. But then the alarm I set on my phone beeps and it's go-time and I don't say any of it.

We sneak back in through the door by the dumpsters, which Vij has propped open with his algebra book—the best use we've gotten out of it all year. Inside, the hallways are deserted and feel over-hot after the few minutes we spent waiting around outside in the cold. The few teachers who are working late have their doors cracked, but there's not many, because it's Friday. We sprint past each door like burglars, which I guess, technically, we are, or we're about to be. When we turn the corner to the sixth-grade hall, I hear a whistle and the squeak of shoes on the gym floor as the basketball team runs sprints. I check my phone. They'll be done in forty minutes. We only need five. Five minutes to do something that could get us both suspended and would *definitely* get me grounded for life if Mom found out.

We stop in front of locker number twenty-three.

"Stop breathing like that," Vij says at a totally normal volume, so anyone in the world could hear.

"Like what?" I whisper.

"You're panting. This was *your* idea. Calm down."

Calm down, he says, like we're just out for a stroll.

"Do you remember the combination?" I ask, still whispering.

He pulls out a sheet of paper and hands it to me. It's wrinkled from being stuffed in his pocket and my hands are shaking, which doesn't help.

"'Twenty-two, seven, five,'" I read extra slowly while Vij turns the lock. I glance over my shoulder. We both hold our breaths while he pulls down hard, like you have to do on every locker, because they're old and dented and basically useless. But it clicks open, smooth as butter. Neither one of us moves. It's been so easy so far. Too easy. Vij saw the combination by pretending to slip a note into the neighboring locker while Chance was unlocking his own.

"Ready?" he asks. He opens the door before I answer. Everything falls out with an almighty crash and I yelp.

"Shhh!" he says.

"You *shhhh!*"

We bend down to gather it all up. I force myself to stop *panting* and refold the bent pages of Chance's history book. While it's most definitely breaking and entering, we're not actually *stealing*. We are not taking a single thing with us. Everybody knows lockers are de facto trash cans. The plan is to see what Chance's got in here and find whatever dirt we can on him. That's it.

Vij restacks the books while I dig around in the bottom of the locker. A half-crushed Twix oozing caramel sticks to a protractor. A bunch of wadded-up napkins from the cafeteria hide in the back. Pretty basic so far, with the exception of a tiny magnetic mirror stuck to the door. Who knew Chance was so into his looks? A ticket stub is wedged between the mirror and the door. I wiggle it loose.

It's a ticket to a Pioneers game from last March. Well that's disappointingly predictable. Of course he would save a ticket from the state basketball team.

I replace the ticket in the door and return to the locker itself. Piles of detention slips peek out from his English and Spanish binders. Coach hates it when his players miss practice. But still, it's no big secret that Chance gets detention. So far this is a huge letdown.

I pull out the binders to see if there's anything left worth noting, and a folder falls out. I pick it up. It's a Star Wars folder, the same pattern as my bedspread at home. Great, we have something in common. I shove it back in before I can think more about it, and his English binder gapes open. Our most recent essay from Mrs. Jacobsen is shoved into the front pocket.

"Check this out." I hold it up for Vij. "Chance got an F—a big, red *F*."

"Sweet!" Vij says, and stands next to me while we scan the page.

It was supposed to be an essay on *The Book Thief*, analyzing the propaganda during the Holocaust. But all he did was write a summary. And he misspelled "Thief" as "Theif" every single time. He also misspelled the name of the main character and, no way, the *author*. He also lost five points for forgetting to give it a title. I flip through the rest of his binder. F in vocabulary. D- on *The Giver* test.

Chance is failing English. Like *failing* failing. And way in the back is a thin slip of paper—a note from Chance's parents saying he's allowed to keep a prescription for something called "Drysol" at school.

I hold it up for Vij, but he shakes his head. We have no idea what "Drysol" is, but I know how to Google. It better be something good, because we're out of time. I pull out my phone and take a picture, hyperaware that Chance could walk out any second.

I grab Vij by the arm. "Come on, man. Let's go."

"What? No!" Vij protests.

"We got what we got," I say, jamming the lock back in place and clicking it shut. "Now we live to fight another day."

Chapter Ten

Trick-or-Treat

On Halloween morning, I lie in bed under my Star Wars comforter, trying to convince myself to get up already and brave the cold. It spit rain all day yesterday that froze and turned to ice before it hit the ground. Then it snowed. Ice. Snow. Ice. Snow. The air was so humid from the heaters working overtime on the bus that Ms. Sherry, our driver, had to pull over so we could wipe down the inside of the windows with towels. It's going to be a slip and slide for all the little kids trick-or-treating tonight.

It's been almost three weeks since we raided Chance's locker. I looked up the prescription. It's the goldmine I was hoping for. But I still haven't done anything with the intel. It swirls in my brain like a tornado of badness, or possibly goodness, depending on how you want to look at it. My last elementary school had posters everywhere that said

"Bully-Free Zone," but the teachers never did anything about it. I was bullied for *years* until Marquis and Cole and Jason came along and provided cover. It's harder to pick on a group. With the info I've got on Chance, I could keep him from ever bullying anyone again. I don't know what's stopping me.

Vij keeps bugging me about it, so I've started to avoid him. Not totally on purpose. I've just been really busy. The garbology business has picked up, and last week Andrew and Peter asked me to join their weekly street hockey game. Things are pretty good for me right now. When I walk down the hall, people other than the newsletter crew say hey. I guess that's why I'm not in a hurry to share what I found. Why rock the boat when it's smooth sailing?

I breathe out, and it forms a white cloud. The extra space heater cranks away in the corner, but it can't fight the unstoppable cold. I check the clock. It's way past time to get up, but Mom hasn't called me. I pull on two pairs of socks and zip my fleece jacket over my pajamas and sneak up the stairs. I put my ear to the door, but all I catch is snatches—

"—not safe."

"—take precautions."

"We," something something "dinner" something "not worth it."

"—finally doing something that matters."

"Matters?"

Something something "miss you."

"Don't—" and then a whole lot of quieter mumbling that I can't make out. I sit on the top step with my arms around my knees. I guess Dad moving back into the bedroom didn't mean their problems were solved after all. I got more sleep last night than I have in weeks, but all of a sudden I'm more tired than ever. I don't move until I hear the coffee grinder whirring.

When I finally creep out and pad down the hall into the kitchen, Mom is standing at the counter in her pajamas with a scarf wrapped around her neck, holding the button down on the grinder and staring off into space

"Hey," I say. She jumps and spills a mound of coffee onto the counter.

"You're up!" she says, chipper enough, and sits down at the table, ignoring the spill. "Did you enjoy the extra sleep?"

"Yeah."

"You okay, kiddo?"

Loaded question. I could ask her the same thing. I change the subject. "Is school cancelled?"

She shakes her head.

"Nope. Delayed until ten, though. Want to do a crossword?" We both look over at the pile of stacked newspapers wedged between the refrigerator and the fruit bowl. It was our Saturday family tradition for so long. We've missed a lot of Saturdays.

"Sure. Is Dad here?"

She presses her lips together so tight, they kind of disappear.

"Just you and me, kid." We've never done one without all three of us, but she gets up to dig through the kitchen drawer and holds up two pens. "Want to be purple or green?"

We finish the entire puzzle in twenty minutes. I get more sports answers than I thought I would. In some ways, it's easier without Dad.

The bus takes FOREVER to get to school. Half the side streets still haven't been cleared, even at almost ten. For one impossibly long stretch on Belmont, we get stuck behind the snowplow going all of five miles an hour. When I run into school, already almost late, I slip on the extra mats Janitor Phil laid out to soak up the slush. I take a hard knee to the floor. But I don't have even a second to feel sorry for myself, because Principal Myer is yelling over the intercom, "Get to class immediately!" and so I hobble toward English as fast as I can.

I scan the room. There's a green creeper from Minecraft. Three girls in Ninja Turtle T-shirts and tutus. A sumo wrestler. A Pac-Man. A bucket of popcorn. And a giant red M&M. I spot Vij, in his usual seat, wearing an orange fleece hat and his ski goggles.

"Hey, cuz." I sit down and tap on the plastic over his left eye.

He lifts his goggles. They've left a big oval crease on his face, but there's an extra crease between his eyes as he looks me up and down. I lean over and look under his desk.

"Are you really wearing your ski pants?"

Vij nods.

"Aren't you hot?"

He tugs at the collar of his ski jacket.

"What happened to *your* suit? I thought we were both going to go in our ski gear."

I push up the sleeves on my red-and-white Colorado Avalanche jersey.

"I, uh, I didn't know it was, like, an official plan or any-thing. Peter let me borrow his O'Connor jersey."

Vij crosses his arms. "Since when do you care about pro hockey?"

"Since O'Connor signed a two-year contract. Peter says the Avalanche have actually gotten good."

"Well, if Peter says it."

"Not just Peter. I think so too."

Why is Vij making such a big deal out of this?

"Look, man, I'm sorry. You still want to hang after

school? We can eat Reese's and M&M's for dinner and watch *Friday the 13th* on Netflix."

He stares out the window. "Don't do me any favors."

I open my mouth, but I don't know what to say. I didn't think Vij would care so much. It's just a jersey. And I already said I was sorry. What does he want me to do, go home and change? When Mrs. Jacobsen threatens the sumo wrestler with detention unless he deflates his outfit and sits down, I laugh and try to catch Vij's eye, but he won't look at me. For the rest of class, I fight a squirmy, seasick feeling in my gut. But it's just a jersey, right?

He's still not talking to me in algebra when Micah shows up dressed like a graphing calculator in an oversize black T-shirt pinned with white squares that have the functions labeled neatly at the top. It's truly impressive and must have taken hours.

"Sweet," I say.

"It's a TI-84!" Micah announces to the room, except no one's listening but me.

"Seats, now," the Crow says, though the bell hasn't rung. Micah points to his shirt and looks at him expectantly, but he doesn't even crack a smile. And then he passes out a pop quiz. Who gives a pop quiz on Halloween?

When Vij is still radio silent at lunch, I've had enough.

I pull him aside before he can get in line. "Look, man, what's your problem? It's just a costume."

He whirls back on me like I punched him. "It's not about the costume, Hugo."

Same as mom, he never calls me by my name unless he's deadly serious or super mad.

I take a step back. "Well, what's it about, then?"

Over Vij's shoulder, I see Peter wave at me from the table next to Jasmine's, where the girls' soccer team sits.

Vij follows my eye and turns. When he sees where I'm looking, he shakes his head.

"Forget it, man, go sit with your *new friends*."

I wasn't going to. I was going to tell Peter I'd catch up with him later. But if Vij is going to make a big deal over nothing, then I don't want to sit with him anyway.

"Fine," I say.

"Fine," he replies.

"Hey, guys!" Em calls from our usual table. She's wearing black cat ears, her Cougars sweatshirt, and a tail. When we don't move, she gets up and hurries over.

"I've been thinking about it and I have an idea for the next newsletter. The problem was that we were too *rushed*. I talked with Mrs. Jacobsen and she's giving us an extension on the next one. It will go out right before Thanksgiving break." She's talking at warp speed and her cheeks are red and tiny wisps of hair have escaped her cat-ear headband. "Lack of professionalism. That's what it was. As editor-in-chief, I take full responsibility. But we're a team, and like you all said—like you *promised*—this next one is going to be great." She stops and looks from me to Vij, finally noticing that something's off.

"I wouldn't put too much weight on Hugo's promises," Vij says, staring me down through his yellow-tinted goggles. "Plus, he has places to be. Don't you, Hugo?"

Vij tips his head toward Peter's table.

"Wait." Em swivels so fast, her cat ears slide a little crooked. "You're not sitting with us? I thought we could use this time to strategize." She looks back at me, the question in her eyes.

"Yeah, uh, not today."

Her shoulders fall and my pulse stutters. It's not her fault she got caught up in this thing with me and Vij.

"But I have an idea for the newsletter!" Do I? Do I have an idea? My panicky brain spits out the first thing I can come up with. "I'm going to make a crossword puzzle!"

"That's—" She pauses. "That's actually genius."

I smirk at Vij. But then it's time to walk away, and all of a sudden I don't know how to leave. I take one step back. And then Em does the same and the space fills between us. Vij watches.

I start to move again just as she says, "I'll have Micah start formatting the space for it," so I turn back.

"Oh, uh, cool."

"Yeah, *cool*," Vij says.

"Well, bye," I say, and then, like a total idiot, I throw my hand up for a high-five. Em gives me a weak slap back and then walks away with Vij following. When they get to the table, Micah and Jack and Gray look confusedly from them to me. I turn before I can see any more. I'm getting exactly what I never thought was possible—a seat at the cool table. So why do I feel so alone?

Somebody decorated the locker room with fake cobwebs and giant spiders. They also covered the overhead lights with paper jack-o'-lanterns so the whole place glows orange. It makes changing clothes so much less stressful. You can hide better. But in a practical sense, it's also just . . . darker. So I don't realize what's wrong until it's too late.

I pull out my gym clothes like I always do. I take off my jersey and tug the yellow Cougars T-shirt over my head. But it won't budge. I tug harder. Nothing. So I shift it around and lift it up to look for the tag, thinking maybe I stuck my head through the armhole by mistake. That's when I see the it. 5T. I have to read it twice. Someone switched my gym shirt for a *toddler's size 5*.

Someone—I can't see who because the shirt is still over my head, but I have a pretty good guess—lets out a high, nasally laugh. "Ha-hahahahahaha!"

I try to breathe in through my nose and out through my

mouth like Mom taught me, but I feel like I'm suffocating. I lower my arms and the tiny shirt falls to the ground.

"What happened, O'Connell?" Chance asks. "Did you finally hit a growth spurt?"

"Where are they, Chance?" I am in boxers and socks with a toddler's T-shirt at my feet. I might as well be naked. I try to breathe shallowly so you can't see my ribs.

"Where's what, buddy?"

"Where are my gym clothes?"

He scratches his pimply forehead. "Maybe check your locker again? I know how messy you are."

They're not in there. I know it. But still I look, feeling the cold air and all the eyes of the entire locker room on me. My regular gym clothes are gone. He must have swiped them while I had my back turned.

"Please," I mumble. My voice is a white flag.

"Dude, I don't know what you're talking about. This looks about right to me." With his toe, he nudges the tiny shirt on the floor.

Chance has kicked my jersey and jeans behind him under the bench. If I want to get my clothes, I'm going to have to walk into the gym in a too-small shirt and my underwear to tell the coach, just like the baby Chance has been calling me all year. It's not *fair*.

He smirks, and some switch flips in me. Shame morphs into anger, and I can't *take* it anymore. I'm the

Garbologist. I'm the King of Trash, Wizard of Waste—everybody knows I'm the one to go to when they need help winning over girlfriends or boyfriends or parents or siblings or teachers or coaches. Who does Chance think he is to mess with me? I rush him.

"WHERE'S MY STUFF?!" I scream. He sees me coming and doesn't move. I pull my arm back. He doesn't look scared, which makes me want to punch him even more. But before I can get in a swing, Coach appears out of nowhere and grabs me by the arm. I jerk to a stop.

"O'Connell," he says, calm as can be. "Principal Myer needs you in her office."

I'd never been in Principal Myer's office. It's smaller than I thought. There's barely enough room for her desk and two plastic chairs. She's smaller than I thought too. You hear her on the intercom and she's like the Wizard of Oz, but in real life she's just a regular person, kind of old, with enormous glasses that take up half her face.

"So, Hugo," Principal Myer says once I sit down in the chair closest to the door. "How are you settling in here at Beech Creek?" Her voice is gravelly deep and roughed-up around the edges.

"Ummm, fine?" We're almost to November. Why ask me about school now? Isn't this about what happened with Chance? Can you get in trouble for *almost* fighting?

Wait. Did she find out about us breaking into Chance's locker? I grip the armrest and try not to look guilty.

She blinks at me. It's hard to read her face through those glasses.

"That's good. I like to think this is a pretty good place to spend your time."

I slink down in my seat.

"I hear you've joined the newsletter," she says then.

"Uh, yeah. It's great."

She nods and puts her fingertips together. It makes me think of that Sunday-school song, *Here's the church. Here's the steeple, Open the door and see all the people.*

The intercom on her phone buzzes.

"Mrs. Myer, Hugo's mother is out front," the secretary chirps. I sit up again. My mom?

"Oh good. Thank you, Vanessa."

Principal Myer unsteeples her fingers.

"What's my mom doing here?"

"Is that your bag?" she asks, ignoring my question. "Got everything you need for the day? Good." She walks me out into the cold, where Mom waits in the car.

"Take care, dear," she whispers before turning back inside. It sounds like good-bye.

It's freezing inside the car. Why isn't the heat on? I crank the dial all the way to red and glance at Mom. She's in work clothes—her favorite cream sweater and the wool skirt with the dots on it that makes me think of Pac-Man. She hits the gas before I finish buckling my seat belt. I'm thrown back against the headrest and then thrown forward again when she breaks at the stop sign.

"Where's your coat, Mom?"

She looks down. "Oh, I must have forgotten it."

Warning bells go off in my head. It's her voice—it's all wrong. My heart squeezes without knowing why.

We make a left and hit the roundabout too fast. A white van swerves to get out of our way and lays on the horn. Mom doesn't react. We merge onto the interstate. Her hands are shaking. She grips the wheel until her knuckles turn white and then lets go. Over and over. Grip. Release. Grip. Release. I don't know where to look, and it makes me carsick and dizzy. My hands shake so I grip the armrest, but it doesn't do anything to still my heart. Something's wrong. Something's happened. Something so much bigger than my fight with Chance.

"Mom. Where are we going?"

No answer.

I punch the armrest. "Mom!"

"Hugo," she says in that robot tone, "we are going to the hospital." And then her voice cracks open, "Your dad had an accident."

My hands go numb. All the adrenaline from my almost-fight with Chance is gone. I shiver. Shake my head.

"That can't be right."

"Hugo—"

"No, Dad doesn't get hurt. He's never even had a fever!"
She hits the gas harder.

I grip my backpack. It's still in my lap. "Take me back to school. I have science next, and there's a lab report due."

"Honey—"

"Take me back to school!"

"Hugo, we are going to the hospital!" she yells. "A nurse called. He was in an accident on the mountain."

"What kind of accident?"

"She didn't have any more information. We'll find out when we get there."

It's when she starts crying that I know it's not a mistake. Dad is hurt, and it's the kind you leave school and speed down the highway for. An acidy taste fills my mouth. I need to throw up. I want to throw up. You always feel better after. But Mom's eyes slide over to me then dart back to the road, and I swallow it down and we don't say anything else.

It takes seventeen minutes to get to the hospital.

The emergency room doors slide open, and I stumble behind Mom toward the nurse's desk. There's a line. A woman with two long, gray braids leans against the counter hugging a pillow and moaning. Half of me wants to shove my way to the front, but the other half wishes I could hide in a corner because if I never find out what happened, it can all be a bad dream and I'll wake up in my basement bedroom and start this Halloween all over again and in this version Dad will do the crossword with me and Mom and I will dress up in my ski gear like I promised Vij and I will skip gym class altogether and then I will eat a hundred Reese's cups with Vij on the couch while watching a scary movie that would get us both grounded if our moms found out.

"Excuse me," Mom says. Nobody turns around.

"Excuse me," she tries again. The woman moans louder.

"Excuse me!" Mom shrieks.

"May I help you?" someone behind us asks. We turn. A man in blue scrubs stands with his hands on the back of a wheelchair. The big guy in the chair holds a wad of bloody napkins over his nose with one hand and checks his phone with the other. I scoot closer to Mom.

"My husband. Sean O'Connell. He had a ski accident. I'm—" Mom stops and puts a hand on my shoulder. "We're trying to find out how he is."

"Okay," the nurse says calmly. "Do you know when he arrived? Or who admitted him?"

"What?" Mom shakes her head. "No. No, I don't know any of that. Someone, a nurse, called, and I came. He was

wearing a blue ski suit. He works up on the mountain."
She can't stop talking. "We just moved here this past July.
He used to be an engineer. He worked with computers.
He's a computer guy. Tall. He has red hair."

The nurse holds up a hand. "Let me see what I can find
out and I'll be right back. Okay?"

"Okay," Mom says, and squeezes my shoulder, but I
don't feel it.

He swipes his name badge at the double doors lit up by
a big red EMERGENCY sign and disappears down a bright
hallway. Mom leans against me so suddenly, we lurch
sideways.

"Come on, Mom."

I lead her to two seats under a window lined with fake
ferns, but I can't sit down. I check the clock. I'm supposed
to be in history class. I pace up and down the row of chairs,
but Mom doesn't notice. Her eyes are trained on the doors
that open and close over and over. I walk faster to speed
things along. Mom is frozen in her chair, but the muscles
in my legs feel spring-loaded. Images of Dad flicker like
movie previews: Dad laughing on the ski lift and pointing
out elk tracks in the snow. Dad with a glob of cheese stuck
to his chin from pizza at Antonio's. Dad's red hair flying as
we race to the bus stop, late again. I follow the tiles and
blink back tears.

When someone does finally walk our way, it's not our

nurse, but a woman with cropped brown hair and a white coat.

"Mrs. O'Connell?"

Mom lifts her hand. A heavy wave.

"I'm Dr. Rothman. I have an update on your husband. May I sit?"

I've got that tingly, electric feeling that happens right before a test or the timed mile in gym, but I force myself to sit.

"Mrs. O'Connell," she begins, "your husband sustained several injuries to the abdomen and right leg. From what we can gather, he was leading a group of skiers on one of the forest trails when he hit an icy patch and collided with a tree. Luckily, he was wearing his helmet."

How is any of this lucky? I pin my hands under my legs to keep them still.

"The leg and—and the abdomen, you said?" Mom pulls her arms around her own stomach.

Dr. Rothman tucks a stray lock of hair behind her ear. She looks too young to be taking care of my dad.

"Yes. He tore three out of the four major ligaments in his knee. He's in surgery to repair those now. He may need a second surgery. We'll know more once the surgeon is finished."

Tore. Ligaments. Surgery. Repair. These words don't belong to Dad. I lean forward, pressing on my hands while she continues, "In addition to the injuries to his knee, he also has two fractured ribs."

Mom sucks in a sharp breath, but my chest seizes up. I can't breathe at all.

"But there's nothing we can do for those. They'll heal on their own as long as he follows his discharge orders and keeps still, which shouldn't be difficult given that he'll be in a locked knee brace for at least six weeks."

"Oh, I'll see to it he keeps still," Mom snaps, real anger in her voice. I can't tell if it's for the doctor or Dad.

"There's one other thing we're keeping an eye on," Dr. Rothman adds.

"What? What is it?" Mom asks, and my nerves rev up, sending prickles down my neck like eels. How can there be more? How many different places can you hurt yourself before you can't be put back together again?

"One of the ribs punctured your husband's left lung. It's a small tear, so we should be able to— Mrs. O'Connell!"

Mom has pitched forward onto her knees on the waiting room floor. Her face is gray, and her eyes are closed. She's trembling and breathing too fast. I don't know what's going on. I don't know what to do. I get down on my knees next to her. She won't stop breathing like that. Too fast and shallow. When I shake her shoulder and she doesn't turn, I start to cry tears that I can't wipe away because I'm afraid to let go of her. Dr. Rothman calls for juice and a blanket. Along with a nurse, she lifts Mom back into her seat. I try to help her hold the bottle of apple juice so she can take a sip, but my hands are shaking too badly.

"Mom—" I whisper, and it hurts. My throat and my body are hollowed out and raw. She looks over at me, and slowly her eyes seem to refocus.

"You're, Hugo, right?" Dr. Rothman asks gently, and hands me a pale green tissue from the box on the table. I wipe my nose. "Hugo, I want you to listen very carefully. I know lung injuries are scary, but the puncture is very, very small. So small that we hope it will heal itself. For now, we're giving your dad some oxygen for extra support, okay?" She says it to me, but she's looking at Mom.

We both nod.

Dr. Rothman stands and shakes Mom's hand and then mine. I can feel the grit between our palms from where I'd pressed my hand against the floor. "I'll send someone to let you know when he's out of surgery. Once he's awake, we'll take you back to see him."

She tucks her hair behind her ear again and smiles. When she leaves, all the sights and sounds of the ER come rushing back. A weary voice pages "Dr. Jordan" over the loudspeaker. Strings of jack-o'-lantern lights flicker above the nurse's desk. The woman who was hugging the pillow is now sleeping across a row of chairs. The smell of hand sanitizer mixes with vomit.

I stare at the wadded-up tissue in my lap while Mom sips her juice. Now all we can do is wait.

Chapter Eleven

Grounded

It's dark when they finally let us see Dad. We follow the same nurse from the ER. It's hours past dinnertime and my stomach grumbles loudly. The nurse passes me a packet of animal crackers. I tuck them in my back pocket for later.

The hallway leading back to the patient rooms is so bright, I have to squint. We make a left and then a quick right and stop at a set of elevators. The nurse whistles while we wait, but I can't follow the song.

We take the elevator to the seventh floor and then follow another hallway to another nurse's station. There's no way we will find our way out again. We get checked in and hold out our arms for the visitor wristbands, a white plastic bracelet that the nurse snaps in place. Then, finally, we turn down one last hallway with a blue stripe on the floor and stop at room 709.

"He's still groggy from the anesthesia, so talk slowly and don't worry if he falls asleep, okay?" the nurse in charge of Dad instructs before opening the door. I move behind Mom. We waited all that time, but now I don't want to go in. The Dad I picture is sitting next to me at Antonio's in his green flannel shirt, picking all the mushrooms off his pizza. I'm afraid to see what he looks like now.

From inside, a voice croaks, "Is that my crew?"

Mom immediately starts sobbing and rushes in, pulling me with her. His room is dim, the only light a single bulb over the sink. I stop just inside the doorway.

"Sean," Mom whimpers, and lets go of my hand to reach him. He fumbles to free his hand from the covers and pat her arm. It makes her cry harder.

"Babe, it's okay. I'm okay," he rasps. I feel like I shouldn't be here. I back up against the door. He catches the movement and waves me over. I make my feet move until I'm standing right next to the plastic bed rail. He looks small under the white sheet.

"Hey, kid."

He reaches out his other hand to take mine, and Mom gives me a weepy smile.

"Hi, Dad." His face is puffy and yellow, and oxygen tubes snake out from behind his ears and into his nose. The air makes a hissing noise.

"How are you feeling?" I've never asked either of my

parents how they're feeling. It's the question they're supposed to ask me. His fingers are cold.

"Well, I've been better," Dad croaks, and then winces, yanking his hand out of mine to grab his side.

The nurse in pink scrubs who followed us in to check his chart looks up long enough to say, "Try not to talk too much yet, Mr. O'Connell. That rib's going to be pretty sore."

Dad opens his mouth, but then closes it again and nods. Mom sinks into a chair without letting go of him. I stay standing, unable to move closer or farther away. We remain like that for a long time in the half dark.

Do you know what goes on in a hospital at two and three and five o'clock in the morning? I do. It's the exact same thing that goes on in a hospital at all the other times of the day. Nurses talk too loud in the hallway. The television at the security desk plays episodes of *Rachael Ray* on repeat. A woman in room 713 calls for more ice in her water every twenty minutes.

I've fallen into a world without time. Nothing changes and nobody sleeps. Except Dad. Dad sleeps like a champ while the nurse in the pink scrubs comes in to take his temperature, and the surgeon comes in to check on his knee, and somebody who introduces himself as the "respiratory therapist" comes in to monitor his breathing. Dad sleeps through it all. Meanwhile, Mom mutters constant prayers of "please" and "thank you" to Raphael, the patron saint of healing, and I play Super Mario on my phone. Not once has she asked me to "check in."

At seven a.m., the new nurse on duty pulls open the blinds. "Oh good, you're up," she says to Dad, who's trying to rub his eyes, except Mom won't let go of his hand. "You are officially allowed solid foods. Are you ready for your breakfast?"

At the mention of food, my stomach growls so loudly, everybody's head turns in my direction at once and my face heats up with the sudden attention. I never got around to those animal crackers.

Mom hands me her wallet.

"Why don't you go down to the cafeteria and get some breakfast?"

"Get me a coffee, will you?" Dad wheezes.

"No coffee," Mom orders.

"Marion—"

Relieved the attention is back where it belongs, I sneak out.

I'm dragging my last strip of bacon through the maple syrup when Mom comes down in jeans and one of Dad's old CU sweatshirts. She looks tired, but more normal now, less like a waiting room casualty. I look down at my borrowed jersey and sniff. It's not good.

"Your aunt and uncle stopped by. There are clothes for you in Dad's room."

"Did Vij come?"

She shakes her head. "They're already off to school."

"Oh, okay." He texted me last night, asking about Dad, but I was too wiped to respond. And also, after our fight yesterday, I didn't know what to say. Andrew and Peter and a couple of other guys texted this morning, so I just added Vij and the newsletter crew to it. I got a lot of "Sucks, man," and "Wicked, bro," but nothing from Vij. I draw a frowning face through the syrup with my fork. We fight and then get over it. That's what we do. But this feels different.

Mom takes a sip of hospital coffee and winces—it's either too hot or too terrible. Probably both.

"I thought I'd give your dad a chance to rest." She pretends not to watch me over the rim of her cup, and I pretend not to notice. "You know he's going to be okay, right?"

"Yeah, I know."

"Do you?"

"*Mom*. Yes."

"Because I didn't."

She starts tearing the edge of her Styrofoam cup in one long swirl. "Not last night. Not for sure. When the doctor was talking and later . . . when I saw him, I still wasn't certain." She stops tearing, catches my eye. "Not until he woke up this morning."

I don't know if it makes it better or worse that she's saying exactly what I was thinking. Maybe better *and* worse. I'm glad he's getting well, but I'm never going to be able to forget that he can be broken. And Mom too. She fell apart. You grow up thinking your parents are invincible, until one day, they're not.

"When you were a baby, I spent a lot of time in a cafeteria like this one," she says, glancing around at the hot food bar, the piles of chips and plastic-wrapped cookies by the register, the people huddled around tables in all different kinds of clothes, from bathrobes to coats and ties to snow gear. I bet none of them planned to be eating breakfast in a hospital today either. I hate it when she talks about how sick I was as a baby. It makes me feel my smallness all over again.

"You were so fragile. We were worried every time you got sick that you might not make it."

"Mom, I get it."

"No, you don't. I'm trying to explain why I lost it in the waiting room," she says, studying her Styrofoam discards curled up like orange peels. "It wasn't that what the doctor was saying was so frightening, though it certainly was. It was *all* of it. The grubby chairs. The smell. Every hospital smells exactly the same. Did you know that? The memories of you in a place like this hit me all at once, along with the fear and the panic and the"—she lifts her hands—"the out-of-control feeling of it all."

She closes her eyes and pinches the bridge of her nose.

"What I'm trying to say, Hugo"—she puts her hand over mine—"is that most of the time I don't think about how often I came close to losing you. And then something like this happens and I remember it all over again. Hugo, I'm so *thankful* for you and Dad."

I don't know what to say. You're welcome? She stands and stretches and saves me from saying anything at all.

"All right. Enough. Help me hunt down some decent coffee, and then we'll find a paper to bring to your dad, okay?"

When I get up to throw my trash away, Mom puts her arm around my shoulders. I don't go in much for hugs these days with her, but I let it stay there all the way up to the seventh floor.

In the end, Dad spends four nights in the hospital. Once he comes off the oxygen, they send us home. Somebody, Uncle Dave probably, has already salted and shoveled the drive so Dad doesn't slip on his crutches. Aunt Soniah stocked the fridge with her famous curry, a vegetable soup, and a tuna casserole that we'll probably eat tonight if Mom remembers it's Friday. And Vij still hasn't texted or called. Yeah, I could call him. But the person whose world got turned upside down isn't supposed to be the one to call. *He* should want to talk to *me* to make sure I'm okay. Everybody else is. Andrew's parents sent a bouquet of flowers to the hospital. And we don't even know Andrew's parents! So why can't Vij pick up the phone? I punch down a pillow on my bed, grab the Xbox controller, and bury the hurt with penalty kicks.

Upstairs, I hear Dad trying to hop around on only one crutch. He is *already* the worst patient on the planet. At first Mom was super sweet and "Here, let me get you a pillow" and "Is it too cold in here, do you need an extra blanket?" until Dad refused to let her help him into the bathroom. Now they're in the kitchen bickering over whether to try to eat around the table (Dad's vote) or sit in the living room so he can keep his foot elevated per the doctor's orders (Mom's vote). I'm just happy to be able to cut off my visitor's wristband. I shake it off into the trash like a handcuff. I remember Mom's words in the cafeteria, about how thankful she is for both of us. Dad's injury *has* to make them realize how much they need each other and then they'll stop fighting so much.

By Saturday, Dad refuses to take his pain medicine even though he's supposed to stay on it through the weekend, and Mom calls the emergency-on-call doctor and puts him on speaker so *he* can tell Dad to take it "or else." And by Sunday, Dad is on the phone with his new physical therapist, trying to negotiate his required rehab down from six months to six weeks while Mom burns a batch of Grandma Sue's peanut brittle and pretends none of us exist.

So much for the grateful, happy family.

Chapter Twelve

6-Across

I am the star of school when I get back after Dad's injury. Everyone wants to hear the story, which has somehow turned into an action-hero stunt worthy of John Cena. *I never said Dad hurt himself vaulting through the trees to rescue a baby deer stuck in the avalanche barrier, but I'm also not in a hurry to correct them.* The cheer squad made me peanut butter cookies.

My teachers also let me have as much extra time as I needed to make up my missed assignments. Except for the Crow. He gave me a totally impossible deadline and then took ten points off for every day I was late. Em even let me skip newsletter meetings, which is a miracle, because I can barely handle sitting in class with Vij, much less extra time after school. We were down to one syllable: "Hey" and "Bye" at Friday dinners. And now it's none. This morning he barely even gave me a nod. I don't care. I've got plenty to keep me busy—street hockey with the guys, at least fifteen bags of garbology projects to sift through, and the makeup homework that is becoming its own mountainous pile in my bedroom. I don't need Vij. I just wish every time my phone pings I could stop expecting it to be him.

The person currently blowing up my phone with texts is Em. Now that I've been back at school for two weeks, she's on the warpath.

She corners me on my way to lunch.

"Two days!" she yells, and I see Jasmine and some other girls look up from their table. "TWO DAYS until the newsletter goes out, and we still don't have the results from the vending machine poll *or* your crossword puzzle, *Hugo.*"

"Em, shhhh. I told you I got it!"

"Well, give it to me, then."

She holds out her hand.

"No, I mean, I'll get it. I will. Just chill."

"Do *not* tell me to chill. Come on. Let's strategize. I've made a schedule to help us manage our time for the next forty-eight hours."

She tugs me toward the table where Jack and Gray pretend to sword fight with carrot sticks and Micah cheers. Vij turns his back when he sees us look over. I pull my elbow out of her hand.

"Em, I can't."

She shakes her head, half smiling. She still doesn't get it. She thinks I'm joking.

"Of course you can."

"*No*, Em. I *can't.*"

Her mouth forms an O and then collapses. I step away from her and toward Andrew and Peter's table with a feeling like wading into too-deep-water. Her dark eyes follow me, but I'm too chicken to look back.

When I walk in the front door that afternoon, the house is dead quiet. And when I say dead quiet, I mean I can hear the clock ticking from the living room and the heating click on and off, because there are no human sounds. For a reason I can't name, I catch myself holding my breath.

"Mom?"

She answers from the kitchen and I jump.

"Hugo, can you come in here please?"

I hurl my backpack down the steps into my room and walk down the hall and into the kitchen as slowly as possible. The holding-my-breath feeling hasn't gone away.

Mom sits next to Dad at the table. The afternoon sun scatters diamonds of red and green and yellow light from the bay window across the floor.

"Have a seat, kiddo," Dad says, and points at the chair across from them.

I sit. But I don't like it.

Mom takes hold of Dad's hand.

"Hugo, honey, we want to talk to you about something, and we want you to hear us out before you say anything. Would you do us that favor?" Mom asks.

"Uh, yeah?" As if I have a choice.

Mom takes one of her deep yoga breaths. Dad gives me the smile he used when I had to get shots at the doctor's office.

"I've had to stop seeing clients here at the house. It wasn't feasible with your dad needing extra help," she says. Dad looks down at the table. "And I wanted to be here for both of you as much as I could."

Last week, an Amazon box showed up on the porch addressed to Dad. When he opened it, there were specially made armrest covers and a cupholder for his crutches. She's accessorizing for him now. Since then, whenever I go into my room, Dad's there, hanging out on my bed and playing FIFA soccer on the Xbox. He's hiding from Mom, which means her plan to "be here" for him is basically backfiring in every way possible.

As if she's reading my mind, she adds, "And I'm sure you've noticed that your dad and I have not been communicating as effectively as we could be." They don't look at each other.

"Sorry about the fighting," Dad says to me, tugging at

the beard he started growing in the hospital and still hasn't shaved.

"That's okay," I lie. I'll say whatever I can to end this conversation.

"No." Mom lets go of Dad's hand and places both of hers flat on the table. "It is *not* okay. And we are so very sorry. No eleven-year-old should have to watch his parents act like children. Even adults don't always have it together, Hugo."

She says it like it's a big revelation. Doesn't she know that every kid in the universe has already figured out that adults don't know what they're doing?

"And we're working on that part." Mom is *still* not done. "We are trying to be better communicators. But . . ." She pauses. "With me not seeing clients and your dad out of work, we can't . . ." she trails off. Something about the way Dad looks away makes my stomach drop, and I start really paying attention to what she's saying for the first time.

"Can't what?" I ask.

"We can't stay here, kiddo," Dad says finally, when Mom can't find the words. "It's going to be months before I can walk on this thing." He leans over and taps his knee brace. "And the doctors say it might be a year or more before I get the strength back to ski, so—"

"What do you mean, we can't stay here? Like in this house?" If we have to move, I'll miss my basement room, but I'm not married to it. We'll find another place in town. I don't know why this is such a big deal.

"We're moving back to Denver," Mom says when Dad doesn't. "Your dad's old boss has offered him his job back, and I can pick back up with my old practice. We really think—"

"Wait, what?"

My ears are ringing. Mom's mouth is moving and then Dad's, but I can't make out the words. We're moving? How can they do this to me again?

"NO!" I yell. "You can't!" I look at Dad. "You *promised*. You're the one who told me you have to *work* for what you want and how it means so much to make this big choice to follow your dream. And now you're just . . . quitting?"

He looks away.

"We weren't looking to move, honey. But when Dad's old boss called with this offer, it seemed like the right thing to do. It's the smart thing to—"

"You *never* ask me what I want. You just tell me what to do and expect me to go along with it like, like I'm your dog and not your kid!"

"Hugo, that's enough," Mom says. "Your father and I are doing what's best for this family. We are trying to make the responsible choice."

I'm still staring at Dad. "So, what? You're going to admit it now? That leaving your old job and moving us all here and making me start all over at a new school was the *ir*responsible choice? Now that I've finally made friends and have a life here?" I will not think about Vij. I will not think about Em and how her shoulders fell when I walked away from her today.

"It could have worked," Dad says, more to himself than me.

"Sean—" Mom starts, and Dad shakes his head.

"I messed up, Hugo." He looks at me. "I should never have left my job. Your mom's been a trouper, but I can't put our family through any more. We'll let you finish the semester. But at Christmas, we're moving back."

"No!" I stand so fast my chair crashes backward onto the floor. "You don't care about me or what I want!" I shout. "You only care about yourselves. You're both selfish!"

"Hugo," Mom warns.

"I'm not going!" The ringing in my ears is deafening now. I can't stay another minute. Another *second*. I sprint down the hallway and out the door.

I walk for an hour, until the sun goes down and I can't feel my fingers or nose or toes. When I get to the playground by the elementary school, I stop. Ice coats the chains of the swings and the seats. I pick up a stick and whack them until the ice breaks and then the stick. I take the steps up to the covered slide two at a time, slip on the last one, and bash my knee against the rail. The pain is distracting and good. Inside the slide, the tunnel turns the world into a porthole of gray. Someone has written *SJ was here* in black Sharpie on the yellow plastic. If someone walked by right now, they wouldn't be able to see me. Hugo was never here.

The cold sinks into my back first and then my bones. They're ruining my life, again. Dad moved us here because he said it would be better for our family. Now he's moving us back for the same reason. How can both be true? I kick the slide and hear the snow roll off the top. It's the diaper in the helmet all over again. They think they're making my life easier when they're just making it *so much worse*. I pull out my phone. Sixteen missed calls from Mom and Dad and one text from Andrew, asking if I can come over tomorrow after school. No text from Vij. My stomach clenches, and the tears I didn't cry at home threaten to sneak out now. I start to type something to Vij, then hit delete. He'll probably be glad I'm leaving.

When I get up, I'm heavy with sadness and the chill. It's hard to walk home in the half dark. I keep tripping on invisible things. I use the flashlight on my phone. Back home, my parents greet me from the couch. Call me in to have a seat, talk things out. The house smells like rice and beans and enchiladas. My favorite. I walk straight past them to the basement. There's nothing to "talk out"— they've made their choice.

* * *

The next day at lunch, I sit by myself at a table in the corner. I can feel Vij and everyone staring at me from across the room, but I don't look up. What's the point? Why go to the trouble of apologizing for yesterday if I'm going to be gone in a few weeks anyway?

I walk as slowly as possible to gym because the wobbly Jell-O feeling that started in my head this morning when I woke up and remembered that we're moving has sunk to my shoulders and all the way down into my legs. I couldn't move faster if I wanted to, which I don't.

I turn the corner outside the band room and run straight into Chance. My head actually bounces off his shoulder.

"Whoa, little buddy!"

"Sorry," I mumble.

"What's the hurry?" He smirks. "Is it shorty plays shortstop day in gym?"

His two friends, fellow basketball players, laugh. I veer left to go around him, but he moves to block my path.

"Get out of my way, Chance."

"Somebody's a little feisty today," he sneers. There's a brown speck of food on his front tooth.

When I don't respond, he raises his hands and steps aside. I walk around him.

"Better learn to watch where you're going," he laughs. "You don't want to end up like your dad!"

"Don't talk about my dad!" I shout.

"Ohhhh, somebody's got daddy issues," he says, each syllable a punch. He laughs louder while he walks away, and it echoes down the hallway. After he's out of sight, I wrap my arms around my stomach and squeeze tight to try to hold the pieces of myself together.

I don't go to gym. I tell Nurse Ruby I might throw up, which is true, and she calls Mom to come get me. Mom feels my forehead, which isn't hot, and asks me how I feel. I slump against the seat and don't answer. When I get home, Dad asks me if I want to watch hockey, but I slink down to my room instead.

I lay on my bed, staring at nothing. Chance is right. Me and Dad are the two biggest losers in town. Life's going to keep kicking us unless we give in and accept defeat. Our one job is to keep our heads down. Forget seizing the day. It's about surviving the day. In just over a month, I'll be out of here and I'll go back to Denver. I'll hide behind Marquis and Jason and Cole, if they'll have me again, and I'll make it through middle school and then high school and then I'll go to any college that will give me a scholarship and then I'll get a job and I'll leave the house in the morning and come home at night and in the middle I'll do whatever my boss tells me to do and every day will basically be the same for the rest of my life. And it'll be fine. Just fine.

My phone buzzes next to my ear. It's a text from Andrew.

He made starting point guard on the basketball team.

He sends me twelve fist bumps and a "Thx for the help, man!"

I sit up.

I never did anything anyone would remember me for back in Denver. I was a champ at blending in. But here, I'm Hugo O'Connell, the Garbologist, master trash reader and manipulator of fortunes. I'm a hero—a hero who has still not used his most profitable piece of information. Locker number twenty-three still needs to be aired out.

I move to my desk and open my laptop. I hear Mom and Dad walking around upstairs, creaking footsteps, the TV turning on and off, a flushing toilet. Eventually the noises stop, but I don't. By two in the morning, I hit send. My head pulses and aches, but it's that good ache like from playing too many video games. I lean back in my chair and breathe slowly through my nose. There's no going back now. If I'm going down, I'm going down swinging. It's time for the Garbologist's grand finale.

I wake up in a puddle of drool at my desk. For a beautiful few seconds, I don't remember what I've done. Then it hits me. And I can only think one thing: *Em*. What is this going to do to Em? Last night it seemed like the perfect revenge. But it's not just Chance who's going to get hit by this. It's Em, too, and the entire newsletter crew. With a feeling like falling, I realize I just torpedoed my friends.

I check the time. I've overslept. But maybe it's not too late. Maybe I can fix this? Heart pounding, I sprint up the stairs where Mom is toasting waffles.

"Mom, you've got to drive me to school."

"Why?" she asks. "I thought you were sick."

"What? No, I'm fine." I tug my jacket on and try to shove my feet into both shoes at the same time, which is as complicated and unproductive as it sounds. I fall into Mom with an "oof," and she pushes me into a chair.

"Sit down. What's the hurry? Why can't you take the bus?"

"Mom, no! I have to get there, like, ten minutes ago!" She puts her hands on her hips. Why won't she just get in the car? I huff and she crosses her arms. I breathe slowly through my nose and try again. "Mom, listen. The newsletter comes out today and it's only the second one and it's *really* important to me and my friends." I cringe. My friends. Can I even still call them that?

She untucks my hood from my jacket and I shift from foot to foot. *Come on.*

"All right. But take a waffle with you."

The waffle sits in my lap, uneaten. Mom drives exactly the speed limit. I lean forward until the seat belt locks, but I can't get us there any faster. We pull in just ahead of the bus.

The front steps are covered in grainy pieces of salt,

and I slip but grab the rail at the last second. The school is empty. I've made it just in time. I race down the hallway, shoes squeaking in the silence, and grab hold of Mrs. Jacobsen's door.

"Mrs. Jacobsen!"

She spins around in her chair. "Hugo! You're here early."

"Mrs. Jacobsen, don't print the newsletter! I, uh, made a mistake. There's something I need to change."

"Well, Hugo, I appreciate your diligence." She lifts her glasses into her hair, *so slowly*, as I dance in place. "But I'm afraid it's too late. Emilia decided lunch was not the optimal time for distribution. I slipped them in the lockers myself just a few moments ago."

"But—can't we take them out?"

The sounds of school are beginning—laughing, yelling, backpacks crashing, lockers clanging.

Mrs. Jacobsen smiles at me kindly, and I turn to walk back out the door.

It's too late.

My heart is rocketing around my ribcage like a pinball. My body doesn't know it's over. But my mind does. I tell my foot to move. It does. I plod back down the hall, now filled with people, with my head down and hood up.

"Hugo! I can't believe you did it!"

Em gives me a million-dollar smile when I get to my

locker. She thinks I came through. My heart shudders to a stop. It's game over.

"I'm so sorry I doubted you. I—" She stares down at her shoes. "I thought you didn't have time for us, for me, anymore."

Now it's my turn to look down. *Em* is apologizing to *me*. Hot tears make the linoleum go blurry.

"But you did it! Just like you promised on the mountain."

Then she leans in and kisses me on the cheek. It is the best and worst feeling in the world, because she has no idea I'm about to break every promise I ever made to her. I'm not a good friend. I'm not a friend at all. I can't look at her. I'm not sure I will ever be able to lift my head again. She doesn't seem to notice, though. She's celebrating our "victory."

"I didn't have time to check the puzzle myself, since Micah had to send it straight to Mrs. Jacobsen, but I know it will be great. And see?" She turns me around toward the crowded hallway. "Everyone's actually *reading* it this time."

She's right. I watch with a sinking feeling as people cluster around our *Paw Print*. Most of them have already flipped it over to the back and are pulling out pencils and gel pens to do the puzzle. How could I not have thought about what this would mean for Em? I just wanted revenge on Chance, and I figured if I put my name on it for the world to see, I'd get the credit and the blame. But it's *Em's* newsletter. If I go down, she's going with me.

"Listen, Em, there's something I have to tell—"

"Dude! Did you see? Our letter's *crushing* it!" Gray says, running up and clapping me on the back so hard I fall forward into Em.

Em gives me another huge smile, and for the zillionth time in two days, I want to puke. There's no way I can tell her—not when she's looking at me like that.

"I better go. I'm gonna be late for class," I say, and walk away from their celebration, because it's only a matter of time before it turns to grief.

Vij won't look at me when I sit down. I know he already knows. He would be the first one to check the puzzle because he's learned not to trust me by now. The whispers start two minutes into first period. Mrs. Jacobsen is explaining the research project we're supposed to start after Thanksgiving break, but no one's listening. They're passing the newsletter back and forth under their desks. After class, Vij brushes by me on his way out, and our eyes accidentally meet. I open my mouth to say something— *Sorry*, and *I take it all back*, and *Please, talk to me, you're my cousin*. But he keeps walking, shaking his head as he disappears out the door.

* * *

Em is already at our table when I get to lunch. She won't look at me. Micah and Gray and Jack and Vij, too.

"Em, I'm sorr—"

"Don't. Just—don't." Her voice is full of tears.

I sniff back tears I don't have a right to cry. And then I turn, shoulders hunched in shame, and make my way to an empty table all the way in the corner.

But to some people, I'm a hero. Thomas, the eighth grader who has never once spoken to me but is now dating Jasmine, thanks to me, passes by and tosses me a balled-up copy of the newsletter. "Nice work, Garbologist," he chuckles, and I cringe. I unfold it and press it flat on the table and make myself read the crossword title: *Taking Chances*.

Six-across: *This bball player isn't worth the RISK. Still unsure? Why don't you HAZARD a guess.* And there it is, filled out in Thomas's green pen.

C H A N C E

That's not even the worst one.

Twelve-down: *The class 6-across is currently failing.*

E N G L I S H

Eight-down: *The book 6-across couldn't spell.*

T H E B O O K T H I E F

I groan out loud. I thought I was so clever, connecting the two answers with the E in "English."

Four-across: *The most important (but ineffectual) prescription drug in our bball player's life.*

D E O D O R A N T

When I found out Drysol was a prescription deodor-ant, it seemed too good to be true. But now I'm looking at twenty-four clues, and every single answer is either about how Chance can't read or spell or smells or is huge because he's actually been held back three times (not true, that I know of). This is so much worse than him switch-ing out my gym clothes or even making fun of Dad. So. Much. Worse. I lift my head just enough to peek across the cafeteria. There he is, sitting with all the basketball guys as usual. But no one's talking to him. He's hunched over his tray, not eating. His is the only table without a *Paw Print*.

I try to remember all the things he's said to me over the last few months: calling me "tiny" and "little guy" and "shorty"; and all the things he's done: hitting Micah with the snowball, throwing Em's newsletter in the trash, nail-ing me in the face with a dodgeball; and even more than that, what he said about Dad. It was all terrible, right? And I'm the Garbologist! I can finally use my power to right the wrongs! I crumple the puzzle and push it away along with my lunch. So why do I feel smaller than ever?

I don't even make it out of the cafeteria before I get called over the intercom to report to Principal Myer's office. They call Chance, too. As I'm leaving, a team of teachers comes in with trash bags. They march up and down the aisles, collecting the newsletters. When the

Crow sweeps a pile into the recycle bin by the exit, I see Em wince and it hollows me out.

Chance gets to the office one step ahead of me. The secretary informs us that both our parents have been called and asks us to take a seat. There are four gray chairs outside Principal Myer's office. Chance takes the one farthest from me. When the phone rings and the secretary turns away to answer it, I whisper, "Chance," and swallow my fear.

He pulls out his phone and starts texting.

"Chance," I say a little louder. "I'm really sorry." If he hears me, he never looks up. I don't even know if it matters. "I'm sorry" can't erase all the other terrible words I used on him. I sink down in my seat and wish I could disappear.

Our parents arrive at almost the exact same time, Mom marching at full speed and Dad hobbling behind her on his crutches. Chance's dad looks just like him, hulking and meaty. His mom is tiny, though, swallowed up in a white puffer coat that goes all the way to her ankles. "Is this the kid who did it?" Chance's dad barks as we wait for the secretary to bring in extra chairs to Principal Myer's office.

"Marshall," Principal Myer begins, "I called you here to discuss the incident. Why don't you let me lead?"

"I just don't understand," Chance's mom jumps in, her voice nasally like her son's. She glances over at me. "How did this boy even gain access to the newsletter?"

"Well, as I said in our phone call, it is student-run," Principal Myer says.

"What, you don't have some sponsor, a teacher in charge? These kids"—Mr. Sullivan gestures at me—"are doing whatever they feel like and bullying *my* son for no other reason than because they *can*?"

I've heard the word a million times, but it's never been about me. Is that what I am now? A bully? I rub my face and then keep my hands on my head.

"The students did have a supervisor. And since our discovery of the inappropriate material in the newsletter, I have spoken with her as well as some of the other teachers whom your son and Hugo share. I've also spoken to several students to try to piece together the full picture of what we're dealing with here. And I must say . . ." She pauses, folding her wrinkled hands over each other. ". . . that I have heard some interesting things—on *both* ends."

With a sense of doom like clouds rolling in, I realize that everything that's gone on between me and Chance is about to come spilling out.

"What does that mean?" Mom asks.

"It means that Chance seems to have been bullying Hugo as well for some time now in regards to . . ." (Long pause in which I want to hide under my chair.) ". . . his size."

"How did we not know about this?" Dad says, shifting his crutches against his leg.

"There was also an incident during gym, something with a dodgeball?" Principal Myer says, turning to Chance, who finally lifts his head.

"*That's* how you hurt your nose?" Mom asks me.

"That was an accident," Chance protests.

"And the name-calling?" Principal Myer prompts. When Chance doesn't answer, she unfolds her hands and places them flat in front of her. "Regardless, none of it warrants Hugo's crossword. Publishing personal information about a student in order to embarrass him is inexcusable. And class records, failing or otherwise, are sealed."

"You're failing a class?!" Mr. Sullivan yells, and places a heavy hand on Chance's neck. Chance winces. "I did not raise you to act like a *fool*," he mutters in Chance's ear—loud enough for all of us to hear. Suddenly, having to shove Dad off my bed for playing video games doesn't seem so bad.

"Yeah, but he broke into my locker," Chance mumbles.

"You what?!" Mom's voice could cut glass.

Chance points at me. "He digs through people's trash. And I think he dug through my locker."

"It was an experiment in garbology," I explain.

"That's not a thing," Chance's dad says.

"It is too a thing! My mom told me!"

All heads swivel to Mom, who sighs and rubs the bridge of her nose. "It's a branch of sociology." She turns to me. "However, this was *not* its intended use. We will talk about this when we get home."

Principal Myer crosses her arms and leans back. "It seems to me that there has been inappropriate behavior on both ends. I only wish," she says, gazing at me and then Chance until we both hunch down in our seats, "that someone had come to me earlier, before the situation escalated. Unfortunately, that was not the case, and so here we are."

Mrs. Sullivan sniffs and pulls a Kleenex from her purse. Dad's good knee bounces up and down.

"As you know," Principal Myer continues, "we have a no-tolerance policy when it comes to bullying, and since it seems both parties were in error, both Chance and Hugo will be suspended for two days."

"What? That's idiotic!" Mr. Sullivan snarls.

Principal Myer ignores him. "As Thanksgiving break begins tomorrow, the suspension will take place the Monday and Tuesday when we return. Now," she says, holding up her hands before Mr. Sullivan can saying anything else, "I trust you boys will take this time to think about what you have done and consider how you might be better citizens of the school when you return." She waits until both Chance and I meet her gaze. "The world is tough enough, gentlemen. We need you to be the good guys."

We don't talk in the car. Outside the window, the sky is a heavy gray blanket and the trees wave hello in the wind with their black branches. Mom takes my jacket from me when we get home and steers me toward the couch. Dad hobbles in on his crutches behind us. We sit in a small, sad circle.

"I'm sorry!" I yelp before they can start.

Mom rubs her eyes and leans forward with her elbows on her knees. "Why, Hugo? I just want to know *why*?"

"Was it retaliation?" Dad asks. "For the bullying?"

"No." Mom holds up a hand before I can open my mouth. "Nothing is worth that."

"What I want to know is where was your gym coach when the dodgeball almost broke your nose?" Dad thumps his crutch on the floor for emphasis.

"You should have talked to us if someone was torment-ing you," Mom adds, "instead of trying to handle it on your own."

"I wasn't trying to *handle it on my own*. I was just—" I run my hands over my head, and I can feel my hair stand at attention like Dad's. "I was upset, okay, about having to move and—" I look at Dad's leg, one red fuzzy sock pulled over his foot below the knee brace. "Chance said something about Dad, and I just—" I'm not telling it right. "Dad, you're the one who says to seize the day, right?"

Mom gives him a look that says, *See what you've done?*

But that's not what I want to say either. I try again. "Mom, you're always telling me to think about the 'why,' not the 'what,' right? When Vij and I looked though

Chance's locker, I was just trying to figure out why he was being the way he was, you know?" I don't tell her Dad was a little right—I was also desperate for revenge.

"You *and* Vij broke into his locker?"

I forgot they didn't know that part. Mom looks like her head is going to explode. She'll call Aunt Soniah. I wrap my arms around my knees. Now Vij will have one more thing to hate me for.

They need to know I'm the only one to blame. And if they're ever going to understand, I have to go back to the very beginning. I start with the Crow's trash and Adra's fruit erasers and Andrew, who just wanted to get on the basketball team, and how I became the Garbologist. It takes a long time. When I finish, it's dark out.

"But, Hugo," Mom says finally, "I only told you about garbology to get you to take care of your things."

"I was trying to do something *important* before you take me away. Again."

"Son, harassing some kid about not being smart isn't doing something important. It's the opposite. It's petty," Dad says, shaking his head.

I hug my knees harder. He's right. The garbology was supposed to be about helping people. But then it made me cool and I forgot about that. And I ditched my friends and now I've got nobody and nothing and we're moving and I can't even call my cousin to complain about it all.

Mom tries to put her hand on my back. I jerk away.

"Hugo, honey—"

I hop off the couch and retreat to my room. At the door to the basement, I hear Dad say, "Let him go, Marion."

Chapter Thirteen

Home for the Holidays

I stay in my room until I am forced out of hiding on Thanksgiving Day to make an appearance at my aunt and uncle's house for the big holiday meal. I turned my phone off two days ago and left it that way so I don't have to see how many people *aren't* trying to contact me.

Now I'm sitting next to Vij in a starched collared shirt while Uncle Dave saws through the turkey and Vij's older sisters, who are home from college, sit across the table, typing on their phones and ignoring us all. Adra is next to Vij, her hair pinned up in a giant purple bow. She keeps touching it like she wants to yank it out. No one looks particularly happy. News of our move has not gone over well.

I spin the turkey-shaped napkin ring. It clatters onto my empty plate. The sound is deafening in the unusual silence. We've never been a quiet family, until now. More than anything, I want to nudge Vij and make fun of Uncle Dave's "Gobble Gobble" tie, and then together we'll figure out a way to hide the cranberry sauce Mom burned under our candied yams, and then later we'll go out in the backyard and pretend to play football, but really we'll play Minecraft on our phones. That's what's supposed to happen.

After an uncomfortable lunch that ends with Aunt Soniah offering with fake cheer to help Mom look up houses in Denver on Zillow, we are dismissed. Vij goes out the back door, and after a few seconds of hesitation, I follow. I find him sitting on the back steps, kicking a pile of slush with his loafers.

"Your mom's going to murder you if you scuff those," I say, and force myself to laugh. It's never been this hard to talk to him before. We'd fight, but we'd never get *awkward*.

"Yeah, probably."

We sit in silence, the trees occasionally cracking from ice thawing on the branches. He stares at his hands without moving. I've never seen him so still for so long. I can't take it anymore.

"I'm *so* sorry," I whisper. My pulse hammers in my ears.

He doesn't say anything back. I deserve that. I close my eyes and keep talking.

"I can't believe I was such a selfish jerk to all of you."

"To all of . . . *us*," he says. I open my eyes. He's shaking his head.

"To you, Vij. I'm so sorry I was such a jerk to *you*."

"You didn't even call me after your dad got hurt. You *group-texted* me, man."

"I know! I know! And I ditched you to hang out with Peter and Andrew and those other guys because . . ." I wince. This next part's the worst.

"Because?"

"Because I liked the attention. I've never been cool, and it feels like you and Mom and everybody else are always having to baby me because I'm so small. But with all the garbology stuff, I finally felt important, big in that way, at least. You know?" Saying it out loud hurts. But it's a good hurt, like ripping off a Band-Aid, because at least it's done.

I glance over at Vij, who is shaking his head again.

"Stop shaking your head at me, Vijay. I'm trying to apologize."

"Don't call me Vijay. You sound like my mother," he says. But he's laughing, and I take the first deep breath I've taken in weeks. The cold air cleans out my lungs, and I feel like I could run a marathon.

"I was shaking my head because you don't know what you're talking about." He kicks my foot, definitely scuffing his church shoes. "We've always had fun, haven't we, man?"

"Yeah," I admit.

"It was never about being cool or uncool."

"I know."

"And now you're seriously going to have to apologize to Em and everybody else, because you tanked the newsletter."

"I know," I groan.

"Dude, you made your filthy, trash-covered bed, and now you're gonna have to lie in it."

I punch him in the shoulder. He punches me back. The marathon feeling is still there. Vij and I are friends again.

He rubs his shoulder. "I can't believe you're really moving."

I look out toward the yard, because it's too much to think about.

"I know."

It's strangely warm out on December 2, the first day back to school after my suspension. The snow is turning to slushy puddles in the bright sun when Mom drops me off out in front of school half an hour early. I told her I needed time to get all my stuff together, but really I wanted to have a minute to prepare before facing everyone again. This way I can sit against the lockers with my feet stuck out and act like my being back is no big deal.

The halls are empty, just like I'd hoped. But all the way at the end, a door is propped open. Of the millions of apologies I owe, one of them belongs to the person in that room. I take a long, deep breath. It does nothing to calm me.

"Knock, knock," I say, and then regret it, because I hate when people say "knock, knock" when they could just . . . well, knock.

But Mrs. Jacobsen says kindly, "Come in, Hugo."

I hurry to her desk and then can't find the words to start. She watches me from behind her red glasses, and I can't tell if her smile is real.

"Take a seat." She motions to the chair she keeps by her desk for one-on-one conferences. I sit.

"Mrs. Jacobsen, I uh, wanted to say I'm really sorry for what I put in the *Paw Print* and I know you trusted me and I'm sorry I let you down. And, uh—" I should have planned this out better. "And if you let me back on the newsletter, I'll do a real crossword puzzle this time. A good one. I promise." I want to say more, but that took forever to get out, so I shut my mouth and hope it's enough.

"Oh, Hugo. I appreciate your apology. I really do," she says, and smiles, and it *is* a real one for sure. "We all make mistakes. It's what we do *after* those mistakes that makes the difference, right?"

I nod eleven times so she knows we are in full agreement.

"But I'm afraid Principal Myer decided it was in everyone's best interest to cancel the *Paw Print*."

"*What?* No! You can't! I . . ." I trail off. This isn't how it's supposed to go. I've apologized to Vij and Micah and Jack and Gray and everybody else in the universe except Em. And now I'm supposed to make everything right so that when I see her for the first time after my tragic and deeply regrettable behavior, I can promise to make it up to her. But now I can't even do that. No newsletter, no redos, no nothing. She'll never forgive me.

"Hugo, it was not my decision to make. I think what Emilia and you all started was truly remarkable. And maybe it will be again, but now is not the time." She gives me a look. It's the "this is not a debate" look.

This is all my fault. The normal before-school sounds are starting up in the hallway. But I can't go back out there now. I can't act casual when I'm the one who single-handedly sunk the school's first-ever newsletter. I retreat to my seat instead. As class groans on, gravity sinks me lower and lower until I'm eye level with the desk and I wish I could stay that way until the end of time.

I watch the clock all through English and Spanish and then algebra, which makes it easier to ignore the Crow's glare and Chance two seats away. I owe him a better apology than the one I threw at him outside Principal Myer's office. It's going to be painful and awkward and a sludgy dose of misery to get through. But I have to find Em first—the worst casualty in all this. Except when I race to lunch and scan our table, we're one short.

"Where's Em?" I ask.

Vij shrugs. And Gray shakes his head.

"I saw her walking toward the gym after class," Micah says, unwrapping string cheese and biting into it like beef jerky.

I leave the cafeteria even though we're not supposed to. Em is not in the hall or the gym or by her locker. I'm about to give up when I look out the back doors by the cafeteria and spot someone in a bright blue Cougars sweatshirt sitting outside on the track with their back against the fence. I run through the doors and onto the track like I'm in a race.

"Hey, Em!" I yell as I reach her, because my nerves have no volume control.

She doesn't look at me.

"Can I sit?"

Still nothing.

"Okay, I'm just going to sit down right here and talk to myself, if that's okay with you."

I crouch down on the asphalt. It's dry and a little warm from the sun.

"It's nice out here, huh?"

"Seriously?" She whips her head around. "*That's* what you came out here to talk about? The *weather*?"

"No! I just want to say sorry!" I scoot back an inch.

"*Sorry?* Sorry for what, Hugo? For taking out your

personal grudge against Chance in the student news-letter? For never taking it seriously in the first place? For getting it *canceled*?"

"All of the above."

She shakes her head. "You broke your promise."

I drop my head. "I know."

She starts snapping lids onto plastic containers of car-rots and hummus and nuts. She's done with me. If I don't say something else, she's going to leave. The words trip out before I can stop them.

"I will make it up to you, Em. *I will.*"

She stops packing up her lunch and looks at me. The wind blows one dark strand of hair across her nose.

"Is it true you're leaving?" she asks.

I slump back against the fence. She leans back too.

"Yeah."

"Then why worry about it? It's not like we'll ever see each other again."

Her words dig in sharp, like a splinter. She's right, but it doesn't make it hurt any less.

"After they told me I had to stop the *Paw Print*, do you know what I did?" She pulls her knees up to her chest.

"What?"

"I went home and looked in my trash."

"Why?"

"I wanted to see what people would say about me if all they could see was my garbage."

"And?"

"And it was empty."

"Empty? Like a few gum wrappers and tissues?"

"No. *Empty* empty." She rubs her nose. "I'm in charge of the trash and recycling at home. Everybody else is too busy or forgets. So, there was just . . . nothing." A tiny breath escapes. "You've met my mom. She loses her phone when it's in her hand. Between her job at the restaurant and her late shift at Walmart, she's always going in three directions at once. Imagine what would happen if I *didn't* keep everything clean."

Em howled on a ski lift and chilled out for a nanosecond because she trusted me. She let herself relax, finally, and I ruined it.

"Em—"

"Please don't say you're sorry again."

"Okay. But . . . cleaner is better, right?" I picture my own trash, overflowing with Coke bottles and broken pens and somewhere, in all of it, my hospital wristband. A waterfall of junk and things I'd like to forget.

"No, Hugo. Because what does that say about me?"

"It says you are *very* responsible and a budding environmentalist?"

"No. I mean, yes, I am those things. But I'm also not making a mark. The newsletter was at least something *tangible* that people would remember me for and that might actually make a difference." She turns to me. "You know they're actually getting those water bottle stations for the locker rooms after Vij wrote that piece?"

"No way."

"Yeah. At least we did one good thing," she says, but she sounds defeated. My stomach tightens. I did this.

"Em, you know the garbology thing is mostly just guessing, right? It's not like you throw a Nutri-Grain wrapper in the trash and that's, like, the defining characteristic of your personality."

"I *know.*"

"I just mean, you're more than the newsletter." I glance down at my too-big jacket. "Like I'm not *just* small. I mean, I am *definitely* small, but that's not all I am. I'm also amazing at FIFA and pretty decent at skiing. And a promising crossword puzzler."

She looks at me sideways.

"I can also beat anyone in a thumb war," I add.

"I can whistle out *and* in," she says finally.

"Nice."

"And I make pretty good scrambled tofu."

"Eggs-cellent."

She elbows me in the ribs.

"I know the newsletter isn't all I am, but I'm still going to miss it."

"I know."

We sit there for a while. I have no idea if lunch is over

or not, but if anyone's keeping track, it's Em. I pull at the brown grass poking through the fence. A Dum Dums wrapper juts out from between the wires. I wriggle it loose, but the wind snatches it, and I have to run to chase it. When I catch it halfway down the track, Em gives me a polite golf clap.

Sometimes ideas come slowly, like a snowball rolling down a hill that gets bigger and bigger. But sometimes they come all at once, like a movie fast-forwarded to the end.

As I'm cupping the trash in my hand, a wrinkled old wrapper from a pineapple-flavored sucker that hopefully somebody enjoyed, it hits me—my movie-ending, bolt-of-lightning plan for how to make everything all right again. It might be the best idea I've ever had in my entire life.

Chapter Fourteen

The Beech Creek School of Garbology

I tell Vij and Micah and Jack and Gray after school.

"Dude," Vij says, "this could be epic."

"Epic," Jack echoes.

"I'm in," Gray adds. "Let me take care of the photography."

Micah says, "We'll all help!"

They better. Because this is one plan I will never be able to pull off on my own. I find Mrs. Jacobsen Windexing her whiteboard and ask her, too. At first I think she's going to say no, but when I lay it all out for her and explain not just *what* I want to do, but *why*, she says, "Well argued, Hugo. Assuming you ask and get approval from Principal Myer *first*, I'll supervise. But," she adds, "do consider the, ah, smell."

"Yes, ma'am!" I yell, and race down the hall.

Gray finds me by my bus. Sometime between the beginning of the year and now, he's buzzed the sides of his hair and swapped his regular sneakers for Converse. It's harder to mistake him for Jack.

"Hey, I just want to say again, I'll help however I can. You know," Gray says, pushing his hair out of his face, "Jack doesn't even like photography."

"He doesn't?" I'm only half listening. My head is too full of plans and watching for my bus.

"I was the one who started messing around with my dad's old Nikon last summer. But when we turned eleven, our parents bought both of us cameras, and that was that. Jack would rather play soccer." He shrugs. "Sometimes I think *they* can't even tell us apart."

After knowing them for four months, I can hardly remember when I couldn't tell who was who. It seems impossible. But I *do* know what it's like for my parents not to get me at all. I forget the bus and my plans for a minute.

"I'm sorry."

He shrugs again.

"I'm just glad you're doing this. And"—he looks embarrassed—"I have a few ideas I want to run by you, that are just mine, without Jack, okay? Can we talk later?"

"Yeah. Okay. That'd be great, actually."

After my bus pulls up and I settle in the back, I look

out the window. Outside, Gray is pulling out his camera to zoom in on a traffic cone completely covered in ice.

Tonight, while we're waiting for the pizza to arrive, I sit Mom down at the kitchen table. Dad is in the living room doing his leg exercises. Every now and then we hear him grunt and then start counting again. "One, two, three . . ."

"Hey, Mom."

"Hi, honey."

It's awkward and formal. This is how we speak now, post-suspension.

"Everything all right?" she asks, and pushes up the sleeves of Dad's red cardigan. She started wearing his clothes after the accident, and she can't seem to stop.

"Everything's okay. It's good, actually."

"Really?" She looks surprised. I must have been really terrible to be around for the last few weeks.

"Yeah, really. Mom? I want to do check-in."

"You . . . do?" Shock, confusion, suspicion—all flicker across her face.

"I mean, I'm not going to lie down on a couch and let you take notes or anything, but I'm cool if you want to ask me how I've felt since we've moved here."

I fold my hands in front of me on the table. Cool and collected.

"Okay." She nods, wary. "Hugo, how have you been feeling since we've moved here?"

"One," I say, and hold up a finger. "Emotionally, I've been happy. Like really, really happy with most of my classes, and it's nice having family close. I really like my bedroom in the basement." Mom laughs. "Two." I hold up another finger. "Physically." I pause, trying to figure out how to describe it. "I know I'm small and that's probably never going to change, but I don't *feel* as small anymore, if that makes sense." Mom nods, blinking fast.

"Three and four go together," I continue. "Mentally and spiritually, I feel older, I guess? Like, remember Dad's fortune cookie?" She looks confused. I never told them this, but I kept all our fortunes from that first family dinner out at the China Palace. They're in the top drawer of my dresser. "His said 'The man on top of the mountain did not fall there.' I've finally figured out what that means. It means the good stuff isn't always the easy stuff. You have to work for the things that really matter." *Not just things, but people, too,* I think but don't say.

"What I'm getting at is that even though I really, *really* don't want to move . . ." I let that hang there for a good solid ten seconds. "I will be okay if we do." I'm not sure I totally mean that last part, but maybe if I say it, it will be true.

"Right," she says, and wipes her eyes. She opens her mouth to say more, but the doorbell rings and Dad yells, "Pizza!" and I am saved from a deep dive into All. The. Feelings.

* * *

After two days of digging through all our trash cans and hauling it to Micah's grandparents' garage, the little mound of garbage me and Vij and Micah and Gray and Jack have made is only about one gazillionth of what we're going to need to pull this off by ourselves.

"We have to do a social ask," Vij says, sitting on a cardboard box labelled CANNING JARS in Micah's garage.

"No! I don't want Em to find out. I want it to be a surprise," I argue.

"Yes, but do you want it to be a lame surprise or an awesome surprise?"

"I agree with Vij," Micah says, scooting an empty Dr Pepper bottle that had rolled away back into the pile with his foot.

"Me too," Gray adds.

"Fine." I sigh. "But I get to decide what we say."

Vij raises his eyebrows.

"Not to take credit! I just want to make sure we say the right thing, and if anyone gets in trouble, I want it to be me and not you guys."

In the end, we decide to make an Evite. We start with a select few from each grade—the loyal ones who have brought me their trash before and will appreciate the magic of garbology at work.

The Evite itself is glittery gold, and Micah designs a graphic of trash shooting off like fireworks when you open it. It reads:

From trash to treasure!
The Garbologist humbly requests the contents of your trash
for a most epic Winter Wonderland Trash-Extravaganza!
Donate your detritus by the school track next Friday from
4:00 p.m.–6:00 p.m.
Please used sealed bags, clearly labelled.

"No one's going to know what detritus means," Vij points out.

"Of course they will. It's trash. The implication is there!" I say.

"Fine." He leans over and hits send, and I smile, but my mouth feels cottony with fear that this whole thing might fail.

All five of us sit there for a few minutes in that freezing garage, waiting and watching to see who opens and when. One by one, the yeses start coming. And then I notice something else.

"Did we forget to turn off the 'shares' function?" I ask.

"No, we did not," Vij answers. "I left it on on purpose. You said it yourself. We need all the help we can get."

The shares zoom way past our original numbers. Half

the school is getting the invite. I sit on my hands to keep myself from deleting the whole thing.

At 9:08 p.m. we receive a message from Principal Myer, who gave us her okay earlier, but we also sent an invite to to keep us honest. This better work, boys. Because if it doesn't, and you turn my school into a dumpster, you'll be spending Christmas break cleaning it up.

We blink at one another.

Vij taps his chin. "Ominous, yet supportive. I like it."

Micah gives me a thumbs-up.

I put my head in my hands.

On the very last day before exams, Vij convinces Janitor Phil to let us use his supply closet for storage because we're spilling out of the toolshed behind the track. We win him over with three jars of homemade apricot preserves we found in Micah's garage. Here's hoping they weren't from 1982.

The mass of donations from the Evite was insane. We had people lined up around the track like relay racers with bags of trash. And most remarkably, Em still doesn't know. I didn't think it was possible to keep a secret, much less a gargantuan one like this, in middle school, but I underestimated Em's ability to lose herself in her first-ever set of exams. Now I only have to make it until tomorrow for the big reveal. That is, if we finish. The supply closet is feeling smaller and smaller as we race to turn trash into art.

Vij stops winding twisty ties together to say, "Listen, I know I pushed you into the whole garbology thing, and you kind of sucked as a human being when it all went to your head. But—"

"Did I mention that I'm sorry?" My ears get hot, and I glance from him to Jack to Gray to Micah.

"You did," Gray says. "About a million times."

"Well, I really am, I—"

"But," Vij says, talking over me, "*this* is something to be proud of, Hugo. Seriously."

He waves his hand over our piles of garbage that are slowly morphing into works of art, and my ears go even redder because I *am* proud of this. When I ditched Vij and Em and the newsletter and published the world's *worst* crossword, I felt like a worm. But tonight I feel the opposite— big and brave and so dang thankful to be sitting here hooking paper clips together with these guys. Garbology always felt like a magic trick when I tried it before. It was meant to wow people while also making me look cooler. But this is something else. It's the magic revealed.

As planned, Vij and Jack and Gray and Micah meet me on the front steps the next morning. We are rumpled and bleary, but victorious. I can't believe we finished. Mrs. Jacobsen donated all her double-sided tape to the cause.

My parents thought I was up all night at a study group with Vij. If you think about it, it's not entirely untrue. I *was* studying. This is earth science in the most literal sense.

I spot Em coming up the steps, her red scarf wrapped all the way up to her ponytail. My stomach takes a flying leap into my mouth. I really hope this works.

I signal to the guys, and the five of us form a line across the top step. Oblivious, she tries to hurry around us without even looking up. I knew she'd be a bundle of nerves for her very first exam. "Em!" I shout when she tries to duck under Vij's arm. She sees me and then notices all of us standing in her path and narrows her eyes.

"What?"

"We have a surprise."

"Okay, great. Can it wait until after the exam?" She hefts her bag up higher on her shoulder.

"Not really."

I take her arm and Vij takes the other and we escort her inside.

"Welcome," I say as glitter lands in her hair, "to the Beech Creek School of Garbology."

I look around, trying to see it from Em's perspective. Streamers of paper clips and twisty ties hang from the ceiling tiles. Red and green tissue paper, recycled from the "Holly Jolly Holiday Dance" last week, cover all the lights. So far, it looks like a disco at the North Pole.

Silvery balloons, leftovers from somebody's bat mitzvah, float through the halls, filled with the white dots from all seventy-two hole punches in the school. When kids pop them as they float by, the dots scatter like snow.

A wreath of used green demerit slips hangs from Principal Myer's door, which she is standing by, welcoming everyone to their first day of exams.

I'm particularly fond of the gum-wrapper tinsel that hangs from Janitor Phil's mops and brooms, which we turned into Christmas trees. That was all me. I will never confess to the amount of Big Red I chewed to get us here.

Hundreds and hundreds of Gray's pictures line the walls. But they aren't the pictures you'd expect. They're the ones that got cut from the paper because they *weren't* perfect: people's feet, a blurry soccer game, a partially iced-over pond, the cafeteria workers laughing, Vij's puddle of fruit salad, Micah re-pinning the cosine function onto his calculator sweatshirt on Halloween, the eighth-grade debate competition, Mr. Carpenter's giant atlas, an orange traffic cone, Em pointing her finger at us at the lunch table. It's a school yearbook, if a yearbook recorded the food fights and snow days and all the ordinary moments of school life.

At first we didn't know what to do with the pile of half-used tubes of lipstick and mascara people donated, but Micah had the bright idea of using them to paint all the bathroom mirrors with snowmen shouting, *U R perfect just the way U R!* He said it's something his granny tells him every morning. Then we wrote *A+++* everywhere else because, let's face it, we need all the good vibes we can get.

We made a giant menorah out of toilet paper rolls.

And an Advent calendar with old binder clips.

We did whatever we could to turn everyone's trash into something miraculous.

And for the final touch, we taped a special surprise to the front of every locker belonging to a kid who turned in trash.

Andrew has a tiny basketball hoop made out of one of his empty Gatorade bottles to celebrate making the team. Heidi, the seventh grader who's never missed a day of school, gets all her old Latin notes folded into origami stars. Chance didn't donate, but I figured this was as good of an apology as he would let me give him, so I made him a Christmas tree out of old Pioneers programs. I watch him notice it for the first time. We don't have, like, a moment or anything, but he does give me a nod and I nod back.

Even the Crow got something—a giant parabola on his door made out of duct tape and turned into a ski slope. I watch Micah point it out to him as he stands with his arms crossed. And then, the biggest miracle of all, he uncrosses them . . . and smiles. I can see Micah sway on his feet with joy all the way from here.

Em is next to me through it all, and I'm a bundle of jangling nerves, trying not to look at her. If she hates it, I'm not ready to know yet. When we get to her locker, I take a deep breath and spin her to face it. She stands there for an excruciatingly long time without saying anything. Maybe she's mad because I didn't let her help plan the whole thing. But I wanted it to be a surprise *for* her, after the newsletter disaster.

"You don't like it." It's a statement. I'm preparing for the worst.

Silence.

She could at least say *something*.

She lifts the giant snowflake from her locker by its string and holds it in the air so it twirls. I can't read her face through the gaps in its paper.

She leans in closer, squints, and then leans back again.

"You made me a snowflake," she says eventually.

"A bunch of them, actually. There are more in your locker."

I point to one tip of the snowflake where you can just make out: "Editor-in-chief: Emilia Costa."

"You made me a snowflake out of old *Paw Prints*."

I can't tell if that's good or bad. Em lowers her snow-flake to look at me.

"Hugo," she says. "I love it."

"Really?"

"Really."

Her face breaks open into a grin, and she holds it up again. We watch it spin under the red and green lights.

Then she leans in and kisses me on the cheek for the second time in my life, and I am shaken up like a snow globe with happiness and relief. If I fail every single exam, it was all worth it.

"There's more," I say, bouncing up and down on my toes. "You get the *Paw Print* back."

"What?" she squeals, and I hand her the formal announcement signed by our principal reinstating the newsletter and all its staff after Christmas. "Hugo, this is amazing! But how did you—?"

"That was all me," Vij says, jogging up with an armful of Post-it pom-poms. They're from Spanish class. I can see old conjugations on each one. "Myer loves me."

"The phone calls from the PTA and pep club didn't hurt either," I add.

Micah bumps into us, draped in a Hanukkah garland of blue exam booklets. We stand there, shoulder to shoulder, trying to take it in. It's like the four of us on the chairlift all over again. Then the bell rings, and the Crow marches through the halls clapping his hands and yelling at people to get to class. He looks all business, but I spot one of our paper airplanes made out of graph paper sticking out of his back pocket.

I think I actually manage not to fail my exam. When Mom and Dad pick me up at noon, I give them the tour. Mom is stunned. Dad is impressed.

"Hugo," Dad says, turning a slow circle under the twisty ties and trying not to wipe out on the confetti with his crutches. "This is . . . incredible."

I look up and around. This came from people's trash. If we hadn't resurrected it and repurposed it, it would have ended up at the dump. I try not to think about what a pain it's going to be to clean. Part of the deal with Principal Myer was that whatever we put up, we take down, and anything that can be, gets recycled. Most of the decorations on everyone's lockers have been torn off. Maybe they're keeping them as a reminder of their own awesomeness. I hope so.

"I know I didn't tell you about it. I wanted it to be a surprise. See, Mom? Garbology at its finest."

She raises an eyebrow. "So, you'll finally empty your trash can in your room, then?"

I give a shrug that could mean anything.

"Hugo really outdid himself," Principal Myer says, coming up to my parents and putting one hand on each of their shoulders.

"Thank you for letting the newsletter start back up again, Principal Myer," I say. "I'm sorry I won't be back next semester to help with it."

Principal Myer looks back and forth between my parents questioningly. I can't believe they haven't told her yet that we're moving.

"Actually, kid, we want to talk to you about that," Mom says.

Myer winks at me. "I'll just leave you three alone." She walks off down the hallway, running her hand along the glittery paper clip streamers so they tinkle like bells.

"Your dad and I have been talking," Mom begins, and I stop breathing.

"I did some campaigning for myself. The ski shop's computer system is in desperate need of a redesign—the whole chain of retail stores, actually. They need a guy with IT and mountain experience," Dad says.

"And I feel like I've made some progress with my clients here," Mom adds.

"And we both know how much you love being close to your cousins."

They glance at each other.

"We know this move wasn't your idea," Mom continues, "but we want to make this next decision as a *whole* family, so—" She looks back at Dad, and Dad looks at me.

"So?" I say with my heart jackrabbiting around my ribs.

"So, if you really want to stay," Mom says, "we'll make a go of it."

"Are you *serious*?"

"Yeah," Dad says, shifting on his crutches. "We're serious. If you want to."

"You're kidding, right? *Yes*, I want to!"

Then I yell "Epic!" so loud it echoes all the way down the hall.

Vij and Em and Micah turn from where they're waiting for me by our lockers.

"I'm staying!" I shout.

"What?" Em yells.

I cup my hands around my mouth. "I'm *stay*-ing!"

"Really?!" Micah calls.

"No way!" Vij yells.

"Way!" Dad shouts, which reminds me that I am still standing by my parents when I could actually be with my friends.

I know this doesn't fix everything. Now Chance and I are going to have to figure out how to coexist with each other here. Mom and Dad will too. But if this year has taught me one thing, it's that you celebrate your wins.

I duck under Dad's arm and run toward my friends.

Vij howls.

Micah howls.

I howl.

Em shakes her head and says, "Animals." But then she howls too.

Outside, the twins wait for us on the steps, and Gray sets up his camera to make us pose for a picture. Out of habit, I move to the end, but Vij pulls me to the middle. The six of us stand in front of our very own School of Garbology with hole-punch confetti in our hair and grin like fools.

ACKNOWLEDGMENTS

Book ideas, for me at least, tend to come from strange places. Years ago, when I was teaching a creative writing seminar to my high school students, one of my favorite books to use was Janet Burroway's *Imaginative Writing: Elements of the Craft*. It covers everything from poetry to screen writing to character and voice. Buried in the section on character was an exercise involving garbology, the study of refuse to learn more about a society. Burroway asks the writer to create a character sketch by describing the contents of that character's trash. It's a deep dive into psychoanalysis that is loads of fun. As I began to imagine Hugo, I used this exercise to flesh him out a bit, and then I thought, wouldn't it be fun to give him a superpower like this to pave his way as the new kid? And so, Hugo became the Garbologist, Master Trasher, King of Compost, Wizard of Waste. Additional credit goes to Dan Aykroyd's character in the film *Sneakers* for using the same method to do excellent spy work.

There are so many people at Atheneum Books for

Young Readers and Simon & Schuster, that I need to thank, not just for this book, but all the books that have come before and the ones that will come after. Reka Simonsen, my editor, has made me not only a better writer, but also a smarter one. She understands my process and gives the kind of notes that I carry with me from one project to the next. Michelle Leo, Audrey Gibbons, Beth Parker, and Lisa Moraleda in publicity have successfully nudged me out the door and into the world to meet and greet. Amy Beaudoin, Sarah Woodruff, and the rest of the Education and Library Marketing team at S&S have worked tirelessly to get my books into the hands of librarians, teachers, and schools all around the country. Thank you.

Speaking of teachers and librarians—you all deserve endless rounds of applause! From book sharing groups on Twitter to YouTube and real-life book chats to insanely creative wall boards in your rooms and hallways, I am so grateful for all the ways you present books to kid readers. You are wonderful. Keep doing the good and hard work.

To Keely Boeving, my agent through nonfiction, fiction, film, and beyond: We are in this for the long haul. And for this book in particular, thanks for the insight into all things Colorado.

To my husband, Jody, and my three kiddos, Charlie, Jonas, and Cora: Thank you for always asking how the writing is going, even when what you really want to know is if the brownies in the kitchen are for you.

To my friends at Parnassus Books in Nashville: Thank you for supporting all my books and for filling your shop with people and dogs who get me.

Lastly, to all the kids who've ever been bullied: I've been there. It's not fair. It's also not your fault. Tell an adult you trust. And find your people, the ones who love you no matter what.